To Ma

Happy reading!
love
Clare Cassy
X

The Willow Cottage Trilogy: Book 2

'Sunny Side Up!'

CLARE CASSY

Clare Cassy has asserted her rights as the Author of this work
'Sunny Side Up!'

(Book Two of the Willow Cottage Trilogy).

First published in Great Britain 2019
©2019 Clare Cassy

For Jonny, the newest member of our family. And also Noah.
Two very special little boys who we hope will become two very
special friends.

Cover design, photo and layout: illuminati-design.co.uk

Sunny Side Up!

CHAPTER ONE

"I am very sorry Mrs Henderson, but the majority of your ex-husband's assets will go to his wife because their child is a minor, and your children are no longer dependent on you. Did you and Mr Henderson ever discuss this?"

"No, we didn't." Milly answered in a small voice, thinking how very young and unworldly her solicitor looked. She was vaguely aware of what he was saying but most of his words were going over her head.

"Do you have any pensions? Life assurance or savings of your own?"

"No, I was a full-time wife, mother and unpaid secretary, helping my husband gallop up his career ladder. And I've just put seven thousand pounds on a credit card to pay for his funeral."

Her solicitor leaned forward and laced his fingers in front of him on the desk.

"You see, unfortunately, the fact that Mr Henderson didn't make a will complicates things somewhat. Is your house in joint names?"

"No, Jack put it in my name once Magda started getting greedy."

"That's good, because if it was in joint names she could go to court and claim half of your house."

Thanks Jack, at least you did that for me.

She could feel this man-boy's eyes on her as she stifled back tears. If he passed her the tissue box on his desk she'd slap him. Bloody solicitors, making money out of people's misery.

Oh God, they were Jack's words.

"Umm," he said, starting that infuriating drumming of his fingers on his desk again. "You say you have a five-bedroom house in Barnes? My advice would be to sell up and down-size. Then you should have a nice little nest egg to retire on."

He's picturing my house, maybe he's about to make me an offer, swindle a desperate, cashless old woman out of the

*property she's lived in since she was a young bride…
Jack, oh Jack, how has everything come to this? We were
coming up to our fortieth wedding anniversary, we were
going to sell the house, go on a world cruise, retire in
France…*

But all those plans were scuppered when the silly man
got together with Magda; a very pretty Latvian girl, half
his age, who set her sights on him in a hotel bar in Dubai
when he was on one of his regular business trips. Clearly
out for a meal ticket she sealed her passage to England by
getting pregnant. The power of sex.
Jack told Milly everything.

Predictably, the relationship didn't last, and Milly, for
better or worse, took him back. Humbled beyond words,
he returned home with his tail firmly between his legs.
Sophie, their daughter, twenty-one at the time, couldn't
look her father in the face for the first year that he was
home. It was bad enough thinking that your parents had
sex, but your father pulling someone not much older than
you? That was *'totally gross.'* Her two older brothers
became hugely protective of their mother, while Milly lost
a couple of good friends who simply couldn't countenance
her taking 'the bastard' back. Other women in their tight
little social circle clearly felt uneasy when Jack was
around their husbands, because they were all clearly
gagging to hear how exactly Jack managed to get his
geriatric end away.

But incredibly, the silver lining in this bloody great
black cloud was little Zac. Magda and Jack's son, now
seven. Magda, was always more than happy for him to
spend time with his father and Milly so she could have a
break from the exertions of motherhood. It didn't take long
for the little boy to work his magic into Milly's heart. Even
Sophie and her brothers thawed and now all adored their
unorthodox little brother.

Amazingly, Jack and Milly, managed to weather the
storm. But then Jack had to go and die. Dropped dead
from a blood clot while out jogging and Milly's golden

years looked set to lose their sheen.

"Let me know how you wish to proceed Mrs. Henderson… Mrs Henderson?"

"I will, yes, thank you," Milly answered as if on auto-cue. A quick handshake and she was out of that horrid office. She needed to calm her nerves with a coffee so headed for the cafe in Waitrose.

Please God, I won't bump into any well-meaning friends, all keen to offer a shoulder to cry on.

But of course, she did.

Vera Hollis, a particularly opinionated and over-bearing member of Milly's monthly Book club was queueing up to pay for a couple of 'flat white' coffees. Some other book club members were sitting in the corner of the café passing round proposed copies of new novels for their next reading project. Quickly putting back her croissant in the self-service section leading up to the till, Milly fled out of the café into the pub across the road. Her heart thumping, she ordered a large brandy and made her way over to a secluded corner of the pub.

What's happening to me? Running away from people I've known for years like that?

Tears pricked her eyes as she picked up a discarded copy of a magazine that someone had left on a nearby table. In between sips of the wonderfully, restorative brandy, she idly glanced through the 'Properties for Sale' when she came across an ad for a wonderful looking, seventeenth-century ex-coaching inn, trading as a bed and breakfast on the outskirts of Chichester in West Sussex. It had a huge, 'olde-worlde,' country cottage garden, four times as big as hers in West London. Compared to what her house would fetch, it was on the market at an incredibly reasonable price.

Well, she smiled ruefully*, I've had plenty of practice cooking breakfasts and making beds over the years…*

Immediately smitten, she phoned the agent for a viewing.

Then she told Sophie.

"But Mum, you're a Londoner. You're a lady who does lunch and goes shopping with your friends. Besides, you can't sell the house, we all grew up here. This isn't what Dad would have wanted."

"Maybe not, but he didn't leave a will. Even if he had, the lion's share of everything will go to Magda, because you lot have flown the nest while she still has to provide for his child. The law is on their side. I can't afford to stay here Sophie." Her voice quaked as she tried hard not to cry. "Maybe it's time I moved on too."

Sophie's shoulders started to shake as she bent her head.

"Oh, darling please don't cry…"

"That bloody Magda, she ruined everything for you."

"Don't worry about me Soph, things could be worse. She can't get her hands on our house. She's a silly girl, who came from nothing and did what she did to survive. Women have been doing it throughout history…

"Yes, but why did she have to pick on us? I hate her for what she did to you – I just hope having to have sex with a dirty old man has screwed her up!"

"Sophie, darling, please… Your Dad won't be the last man to make such an idiot of himself. Don't think that he never regretted it… He did love you," she added in a conciliatory tone. "You were always his little Princess."

"It's not me, I'm worried about," Sophie snapped as she gave full throttle to her pent-up anger. "So, you're going to bury yourself in the country, slaving over pans of eggs and bacon, tripping over bundles of dirty washing while she's squandering all your money?"

With a supreme effort and not a little bitterness, Milly bit her lip:

Just look what you've done to our daughter Jack...

"I may not like the place, Soph, or someone else might pip me to the post, who knows? But it could be perfect, I need to work. I've just turned sixty and never had a proper job."

"Yes, you did. Don't you dare say that," Sophie's blue eyes flashed with anger as she started sobbing again.

"You're a trained nurse and worked in a London hospital."

"Only for a few years before I got married dear."

"So? Then you brought up us and made a fine job of it. All my friends secretly wished you were their mother, and Dad would never have done as well as he did without you buttering up his clients and cooking all those lunches. Even Nana said so..."

"Thank you dear, but that was then and this is now." Sophie studied her mother.

"Mum, this isn't a knee jerk reaction is it? I mean, we've only just buried the prick..."

"Soph!"

"Sorry... and what about your 'Lumpy Lady Club?' You've been going to your 'Aqua Aerobics' classes twice a week for the past ten years with all your friends, then there's your book club. You love that. You do have a life here Mum..."

"I know darling, but life has changed for me. I either stay here, alone in this house and panic about paying the bills, or grab what opportunities come my way."

"You could rent out rooms? I could come back and help you out?"

"I don't want lodgers darling and you love your flat. You have a life too."

"What about Ben and Jake? Have you told them?"

"No," she smiled, imagining their reaction. "It's just an idea at the moment. Anyway, you know your brothers. We only ever hear from them when it's Christmas, or there is a crisis, or its one of our birthdays. They are both fine darling, busy climbing up their corporate ladders and being young, free and single. Besides, I have a sneaky feeling they would be quite proud of me."

"So, you are definitely considering this 'B&B' idea?"

"It's just a viewing darling. I may not like the place..."

"Oh my God, I can't believe it, my mum running a 'B&B' while all my friends' parents are retiring to Spain on fat pensions…"

"Well, you'd better get used to it, because if I get it, I'll soon get you stripping those beds," Milly laughed, topping up their wine glasses.

"Urgh, you won't get me touching any sheets," Sophie wrinkled her pretty little nose in mock disdain. "Oh well, if you are serious, here's to you," she added, raising her glass. "I would rather you were about to embark on a world cruise but since you're not, here's to my fabulous, working mum."

Seven weeks on from burying Jack, they were slowly starting to smile again. Tomorrow, Milly would be driving to Chichester to view the property. Sophie would have gone with her but she was working and Milly, who at one time couldn't even go to the shops without Jack, was starting to relish doing things on her own.

Chapter Two

"Please don't look at me like that, darling," Milly ruffled her Great Dane, Rufus, behind his ear. I'm coming back."

He hated being on his own but Milly couldn't take him with her. It would take a good hour and a half to drive to Chichester from London. He wasn't very good on long car journeys and he'd be on his own in the car while she viewed the house. Thank goodness for Max, her fourteen-year old neighbour's son, who was always more than willing to earn a few quid by looking in on Rufus and walking him on Barnes common. Giving him a treat to chew in his basket, Milly switched the radio on in the kitchen so he had some company, locked the front door and made her way out to Jack's battered old Bentley. As she settled into the driver's seat, she could still smell the comforting fragrance of Jack's old aftershave.

After tapping the post code for 'Willow Cottage' into her Sat Nav, she saw that her estimated time of arrival was around ten thirty. Perfect timing for her appointment with Holly Perone, the vendor.

Now don't go doing anything rash, this is a big decision. The place might look lovely but, it could easily turn out to be a great big money-pit... Just don't get carried away on a whim, Milly chided herself, as she reversed out of her drive.

The grey monotones of London ebbed away, morphing into the green rolling hills of West Sussex, dotted with lambs and white sheep. Milly's soul did a little dance. This was driving at its best and she felt nineteen again as she sang along to 'Faith' by George Michael.

'You have reached your destination.'
My God its huge! Built in a classic Elizabethan L shape, 'Willow Cottage' was painted an attractive shade of duck-egg blue. Roses clustered around the front door and an array of country cottage flowers jostled for attention in the

sunny front garden. Turning past the black and white wrought iron 'B&B' sign, into a long sweeping driveway lined with Hollyhocks, Milly carefully parked the car in front of a cluster of blackberry bushes, then fished inside her handbag for her small silver compact mirror, Jack had engraved with her initials in London's Convent Garden.

A quick powder of her nose and she swapped her driving shoes for a nice pair of red kitten heels which added a nice little contemporary touch to her rather conservative skirt and jacket. Stepping out of the car, she did a quick yoga stretch to relieve her cramped joints and quickly surveyed the scene around her. The renowned Fishbourne Palace was in the grounds behind the house. The next-door neighbour's garden boasted a beautiful carpet of bright yellow Daffodils interspersed with Bluebells. As Milly made her way to the front door she passed a spacious back garden, split into two distinct sections, one of which had half a dozen or so pecking and scratching speckled hens running around the lawn. What a lovely sight it was to see them roaming about so freely.

The smell of the roses around the front door was intoxicating and Milly would have liked another couple of minutes to savour their sweet scent but seconds later a large, threatening looking dog with a very deep, loud bark bounded to the door. As used to dogs as she was, after all, Rufus was like a mini horse, she couldn't help but feel uneasy around this one.

"I'm Holly Perone." a very pretty dark-haired young woman, carrying a lovely smiley baby, reassured her as she opened the door. "Don't worry about Tess, her bark is a lot worse than her bite," she said, indicating the dog. "It's good to have a big, scary looking dog in a place like this… You must be Mrs Henderson?"

"I am, yes. What a beautiful house you have," Milly replied, shaking Holly's hand. "And who is this lovely little girl?"

"This is Ivy," Holly replied proudly, jiggling her on her hip. Please, do come in."

Milly's eyes were immediately drawn to a wonderful, mahogany winding staircase in the hall. An intriguing mix of contemporary art, antique-looking tapestries and various pictures of country scenes adorned the walls. A small table by the front door was crowded with an assortment of tourist guides. Following Holly, little Ivy and Tess the dog, Milly was led past a large kitchen, dining room and laundry room into a spacious back sitting-room with a very attractive, open brick fireplace.

A large framed photograph of a very handsome young man in red motor-racing gear, spraying a magnum of champagne, hung above the fireplace.

"That's Ivy's Dad, he'd just won a major race at Goodwood. He was one of my first guests and we ended up getting married." Holly said proudly.

"Oh, my goodness, how lovely."
There was also a beautiful wedding photograph of the two of them proudly displayed on top of a Baby-grand piano in the corner of the room.

"Yes, 'Willow Cottage' was a very lucky move for me."

Milly would have loved to have heard more but this wasn't a social visit. Understandably, the young woman seemed keen to get the viewing over. Still cradling her baby, she explained that they lived in this part of the house while the rest of the property was set-aside for guests.

"We're looking for a quick sale, my husband's American and we're moving to the States."
Milly explained that she was looking for a quick move too and was confident her house would sell quickly.

"Right then, I'll show you around the house." Holly said decisively.

Milly loved the kitchen with its long, scrubbed pine trestle-table and matching, impressive dresser, cluttered with brightly coloured china. The dining room was very attractive too. About half a dozen little tables sporting crisp, white linen table-cloths were covered with an assortment of stainless-steel teapots and jugs.

Used individual tubs of butter, marmalade and jam were piled up in pyramids on empty plates.

"I haven't had a chance to clear up yet," Holly said apologetically, "My guests weren't in a hurry to go this morning."

The dining room also had an inviting open brick inglenook fireplace with an interesting collection of antique iron pokers and kettles, alongside a decorative brass coal scuttle in the hearth. An attractive arrangement of dried hops, various brass pans and iron ornaments hung on the wall above the fireplace and a nicely worn Persian rug added a bit of colour and style over a good quality, olive green carpet.

"Guests tell me what time they want breakfast the night before. I don't start cooking 'til they come down. Pointless cooking anything in advance as they are often late or don't come down at all."

Little Ivy's huge dark eyes studied Milly's face over her mother's shoulder as they did a whistle-stop tour of the ground floor. Milly particularly liked the quirky little ironing room with its scrubbed pine, French-style dresser and battered old sofa.

"This iron saved my life," Holly explained, pointing out the specially designed roller-ball contraption in the corner. "I couldn't have kept up with the ironing without it. My husband said it would be more time and cost-effective to have the linen professionally laundered but I actually really got into my ironing using this!" Holly joked, demonstrating how easy it was to feed in a sheet or towel over the rotating roller.

"Yes, I can see this would be a lot easier than using a hand-iron," Milly agreed.

"Well, I won't be needing it in the States, so I can pass it on," Holly smiled, hopefully.
Milly could just picture herself sipping her morning coffee in here, as she contemplated the day's ironing.

A little window looked out on the back garden where

the chickens were pecking about. One was racing around in mad circles with a worm in its mouth. Another bird, its eye on the worm, in hot pursuit behind it. It really was a very comical sight.

Walking back into the entrance hall, they mounted the wonderful, sweeping staircase to the bedrooms on the next three floors.

There'd be no need for any 'Lumpy Lady' classes after a daily workout like this.

"This is my sewing room." Holly said, as they stepped into a lovely, yellow room, on the first floor. The sun was streaming in through a beautiful, stained-glass window over-looking the back garden. A dress-maker's dummy stood proudly in her semi-naked glory by the window with half a skirt pinned around her. Tape measures and cottons reels were scattered around a vintage 'Singer' sewing machine and work table.

"This room used to be a 'Dame School' and there's an old photograph, showing just how it looked in Victorian times." Holly said, leading Milly over to a faded old picture hanging above a small fire-place. A ragged bunch of little children were standing to attention next to a fierce old 'Dame', clad entirely in black save for her white bonnet. "Families paid a penny a week to have their children taught to read and write in this room, by Miss Gibbons here. She's buried in Fishbourne churchyard."

"My goodness, how wonderful. Where did you get the photo?"

"The previous owners found it stuck behind this mantle-piece when they moved in. They thought it would be nice if Miss Gibbons stayed in her school room." Reluctantly, Milly tore herself away from the picture as Holly directed her over to a door in the corner of the room which opened to an outside staircase, leading to the garden below. This, she explained, used to be the back entrance to the school as the children and Miss Gibbons were banned from entering the school-room from the front of the house.

Milly could just picture the children climbing up the crumbling, moss-covered, steps every morning, quaking in their boots at the sight of their scowling school Ma'am. *I've got to have this house. It's wonderful…*

The bedrooms on the next two floors were all named after flowers. There was the pink Wallflower room, the blue Delphinium, white Heliotrope and the mauve Lilac room. And that was just for starters. Milly's favourite was the Magnolia room right at the top of the house; with its sloping ceiling, lovely little window seat and pretty, stained glass window which bathed the room in soft blue light.

"I had that window specially made." Holly remarked.

"It's very pretty," Milly commented, looking at it more closely. A large green Willow tree, under a beautiful blue sky dominated the window.

"You can see why I chose a Willow tree," Holly smiled, adding: "When the light shines through the central panel there is a green glow from the tree. The artist did a good job."

I can just see Sophie here, she'd love this room…

"We put in all the flat screen TVs and changed all the towels and bed linen for white Egyptian cotton. It was all rather garish when we moved in. The previous owner liked flowery bed sheets. The towels didn't match the sheets and the duvets were as thin as dusters. It must have been freezing for the poor guests."

Then, directing Milly over to a large cupboard in the hall outside the rooms, Holly proudly showed off her neat shelves of beautifully ironed, bed linen – all painstakingly labelled into sets and sizes.

"The bed linen was just shoved in here when I came. There was no organisation. So, I'd pull out a double duvet only to find it was a single or a King. Not very funny when you have to keep traipsing back to the cupboard and iron them all again."

"No, I can imagine."

"Did you have any help managing the rooms?"

"Yes, Madge. A lovely lady who wasn't the best at housework but became a life-long friend." Holly smiled at the memory, adding, "She ended up marrying one of my guests. Most be something about this house…"

"Indeed," Milly agreed.

There's hope for a merry widow yet…"

"She married my wonderful Mr Wainright, a regular guest who sold greetings cards to shops in Chichester. They're now running a tea shop in Dorset. It was Madge who did the baking for my little café in the garden… now, where were we?" Holly added purposefully, "Oh yes, the TV's and bed linen all come with the fixtures and fittings as does the bedroom furniture and I've also got a huge selection of mops and cleaning materials I can leave for you," she said opening an adjacent cupboard.

More stairs, and they reached Holly's prize room.

"Now this is the Honeymoon suite."

A huge, four poster bed, dominated the room with a sweet, little Victorian style cherub above the bedstead. Nicely faded tapestries adorned the walls. Milly's eye was drawn to a very pretty sampler which had been carefully embroidered and named in perfect stitches, by a fourteen-year old girl called Eleanor Gibbons in 1869. An attractive, antique, walnut chest of drawers had a pretty bowl of sweet-smelling potpourri on it and there was a lovely, olive green balloon backed chair in the corner of the room. The furniture in this room was clearly a lot more superior than the more functional items in the other rooms.

"You have to watch wedding parties though. They can get a bit boisterous sometimes. The previous owner told me all her good champagne glasses were smashed by one party so I'd advise you to get some inexpensive ones, just in case… Right, I'll show you the Brewery next."

"Oh, that sounds interesting," Milly said brightly, following her gingerly down a perilous, creaky, little back-staircase.

The Brewery, Holly explained was the oldest part of the house. Originally a coaching inn, this was where the horses were rested and beer was served to passing travelers. An attractive modern-day mural of Tudor wenches serving goblets of beer inside a rowdy inn, with boys brushing horses and feeding the dogs waiting outside, was painted in eighteenth century style, on one of the walls in the little entrance hall.

"The previous owner had this painted by a local art student."

It was captivating.

Holly then pulled back the corner of an old Persian rug revealing a rusty metal plate embedded in the floor.

"There's a secret tunnel under here," she said, tapping it with her foot. "It leads straight out to Fishbourne Creek and was used by bootlegging pirates doing their business right here in this brewery with the inn-keeper."

"Oh, my goodness, has anyone been down there?"

"I'm sure over the years a lot of people have tried. But the previous owners said the hole has closed up."

Milly was spellbound. *I can see myself here. And Sophie and Zac.* She was conscious she was just standing and staring mutely at the mural, envisaging all the pirates, rowdy beer drinkers and wenches of yesteryear.

She didn't want to leave and forced herself to go. Thanking Holly for her time and she said she'd contact the agent to make an offer.

Holly could sense that this lovely lady was at some cross-roads in her life. Just like she was when she came to view the house.

"It's a long drive back to London, would you like a cup of tea before you go?"

"That would be lovely, if you can spare the time? Shall I take Ivy?"

They made their way back to the kitchen and Milly happily held Ivy while Holly made some tea.

"Well, it looks like my 'B&B' days will be over soon," Holly remarked wistfully as she put the kettle on.

"Did you enjoy them?" Milly asked, trying to stop Ivy pulling out one of her pearl earrings.

"I did. It had its ups and downs but when I first came here, I was at a point in my life when I needed a change and I definitely found it here at 'Willow Cottage'."

"Yes, well, a change is what I need and fast." Milly smiled, trying to sound upbeat. "I was married for forty years but my ex-husband's assets are all set to go to his second wife."

"Oh, my goodness, that's awful, I'm so sorry."

"It's alright dear. She has a young child and so it only seems fair, the law is on their side. All my children have flown the nest."

Doesn't sound fair to me, Holly frowned. *Married for forty years and she gets nothing. Poor woman…*

"I did get the house. Luckily it was in my name."

Thank god for that…

"Trouble is, I can't afford to live in it. So, when I was contemplating my future over a quiet brandy in the pub, I saw your ad in a magazine someone had left."

Images of herself, in her troubled state, when she first came to view 'Willow Cottage' flashed through Holly's mind. Her heart had been broken by the man she thought she'd spend the rest of her life with. His callous and uncaring attitude when she lost their baby was the final nail in the coffin, although it did lead her to 'Willow Cottage' and a new life.

"Well, as I said, 'Willow Cottage' was very lucky for me, Mrs Henderson. And I think it could be very lucky for you too."

Milly sipped her tea thoughtfully.

"Do you know dear, I have a very strong feeling you could be right."

Shaking Holly by the hand and thanking her for the tea, Milly assured her that she'd be in touch soon.

"I hope so," Holly whispered into Ivy's sweet-smelling curls. "We'd be happy for her to have our house, wouldn't we?"

At least she got the Bentley, Holly smiled as she watched Milly drive down the drive.

Chapter Three

Sophie went with her mother for the second viewing and was equally as smitten with the house and garden. Predictably, she loved the room with the stained-glass window and was blown away by the mural in the Brewery and Holly's tales of smugglers and pirates.

"Would you continue with the café idea Mum? It's a perfect spot with that little stream at the end of the garden. Holly said it was very popular and she could put you in touch with a good baker."

"Now, that would be a nice little project for you Soph?" Milly suggested, hopefully. Her eyes lighting up with enthusiasm. "I can just see you charming all the customers…"

Sophie raised her perfectly arched eyebrows.

"Maybe, in time Mum, who knows? What will you do with all your furniture?" She asked, keen to change the direction of the conversation. "You're not going to need it all with all these fixtures and fittings?"

Milly pondered.

"Put it in storage for you and the boys? Sell it? I'd bring my sofa, chairs, pictures and the odd table and mirror. You know, the 'fluffy pieces' as it were, but I'm not even going to need my dining-table, am I?"

"No, I suppose not."

"So, anyway darling, do you think I should go ahead?"

"Definitely, I can see you here."

***

Eight weeks later, Milly was collecting the keys to 'Willow Cottage'.

"The last owner married a famous racing driver who used to stay there. It was in the local paper," the pretty, young estate agent confided to Milly as she signed for the keys. "How romantic is that?"

"It is rather, isn't it?" Milly agreed, recalling the

picture of the laughing young man spraying the magnum of champagne. "One never knows when one's handsome prince will make an appearance."

"No, I suppose not, here's hoping," the girl blushed. All the best to you, Mrs Henderson."

After a quick handshake, Milly practically skipped out of the estate agents with the keys to her new life.

"Come on Rufus," she called back to her Great Dane, who was happily ensconced behind the dog guard in the back of the Bentley. "Let's go and check out our new home."

Balancing his dog basket and bowls with one hand, she turned the key in the front door.

After a good sniff and very long wee in the front garden Rufus bounded straight past Milly into the hall, nearly knocking her and his basket and bowls flying.

"Thanks Rufus!"

Collecting herself, she walked into the kitchen, put the dog basket down in a cosy corner by the Aga and filled the water bowl. *Well, Jack, I think you would approve.* Milly smiled sadly to herself as she surveyed the kitchen with fresh eyes. *It still feels so odd that you aren't part of all this...*

Rufus, meanwhile had plonked himself down in his bed and was happily chomping one of his toys.

A note had been left on the kitchen table.

Dear Milly,
As agreed, I continued taking bookings for you, which you will see in the Bookings Book I have left by the landline. Charlie Worsley, an actor performing at the Chichester Festival theatre will be staying in the Delphinium Room for three months. I think he is performing in 'Birdsong.' (We often get actors staying for the run of their show). I've also booked in Miss James, who's one of our regulars; a very glamorous lady in her nineties who always comes with her horrid little dog, Fang! Her daughter will drop

her off. She usually stays in the Lavender Room.
A lot of punters come to the door. Make sure you have
your dog with you and get them to sign in with their car
registration number and pay upfront. You don't want any
runners! 'Willow Cottage' was very lucky for me, I'm sure
it will be for you too.
All the best
Holly.

"Right old boy," Milly called affectionately to Rufus.
"I'd better go and remind myself where their rooms are."
Rufus looked non-plussed, more intent on chewing his toy
than exploring his new home.

A rush of excitement ran through Milly's veins as she
flung open the doors to all the bedrooms on her quest to
find the Delphinium and Lavender rooms.
Yes, they do all belong to me! she reminded herself. *Ah,
here they are. The larger double, the 'Delphinium', for the
actor and the small, single 'Lavender' Room for the old
lady.* The linen was clean as were the little sinks and
mirrors. New tea, coffee and milk sachets had been put by
the kettles. The rooms would just need a final dusting and
airing before her guests arrived. And maybe a nice little
vase of violets from the garden for the old lady. *Yes, that
would be a nice little touch,* Milly thought as she sat down
on the bed.

Suddenly a picture of little Zac, at Jack's funeral
sprung into Milly's mind. Magda was weeping and wailing
theatrically while the child, wearing that ridiculous suit,
stood limply by her side in the church.

"God, why doesn't she shut up!" Ben had hissed to
Milly. "We all know she didn't give a toss about Dad."
Milly had quietly agreed.

They were all walking back to the car, after looking at
the flowers by the graveside when Zac rushed over to
Milly and pulled a sweet out of his pocket.

"Milly, I've got a sweet for Dad," he said, slipping his
hand into hers and pulling her back to the flowers.

"Here Dad, here's a sweet for you," he said bending down and putting it amongst some roses.

"Hey Zac," Milly said softly, bending down to his level. "A Liquorice Allsort, that's your Dad's favourite sweet. He'll love that." She loved that little boy more than ever at that very private moment.

Jack always worried about Zac. Most of the time he spent with Magda he was holed up in his room playing on his playstation. She didn't take him to the park or the play-ground and he never wanted to go home after staying with Milly and Jack.

I'll phone Magda, arrange for Sophie to bring him down to stay. He'd love it here.

As she plumped up the cushions in the Lavender Room, her thoughts turned to the new family in her house in Barnes. A charming American couple with three boisterous boys. It had been incredibly painful packing up, walking out of the house and handing over the keys. Predictably, Milly's boys were too busy to help, but in all truth, she didn't want anyone there. Not even Sophie. This was something she had to do on her own. It was up to her to dismantle the memories. To turn that page of her history. Every picture and every ornament told its own story as she carefully dusted and packed them in boxes. That ridiculously over-priced picture Jack bought in Venice. All their books cluttering up the house that she'd refused to give away, and the little trinkets and cards the children had made at school over the years. She'd kept them all. Mountains of old photos, school projects and reports by the dozen. Separating them into named piles for each child, Milly had carefully boxed them away.

Because she'd bought a lot of the fixtures and fittings at 'Willow Cottage' she sold most of her furniture. She would never forget the look on Sophie's face when she turned up unexpectedly one day and watched that frightful woman, smugly carrying out their beautiful old walnut dining room table and chairs that Milly had sold to her for a song. Sophie was watching her childhood disappear through the door...

Back to reality.

Oops, I've been sitting on the bed.

Brushing away the creases, she made sure the fringes on the rug were still properly straightened and combed with the old-fashioned perming comb that Holly said was always kept hidden above the door frame, expressly for that purpose.

But as exciting as this new venture was, Milly couldn't ignore the well of loneliness seeping into her stomach. She was alone in a huge old house. There were so many rooms, she wasn't familiar with exactly where they all were. Yes, the honeymoon suite, two double and one single room were on the top floor. Two 'family' rooms with a double and a couple of single beds in each, were on the middle floor, along with one or two other rooms. Then, there was the Brewery, which had a twin and something else. But if someone had asked if they were the 'Delphinium', the 'Magnolia' or 'Foxglove' rooms, Milly just wouldn't have had a clue.

After a lot of deliberation, she decided that like her predecessors, she would sleep in the back part of the house which was safely tucked away from the guests. After all, it wouldn't feel comfortable sleeping next-door to different strangers each night. Besides which, these rooms didn't come with any fixtures or fittings so Milly could keep some of her old furniture. Her antique dressing table and free-standing wardrobe and Sophie's old single bed for the bedroom and other bits for the adjacent sitting room.

Yes, they would fit in nicely.

Rufus was decidedly unsettled when they went into the back part of the house later that night. He clearly didn't like being in the sitting room and followed Milly every time she walked out of the room. He seemed particularly hesitant about going into the bedroom.

"You can come in Rufus, this is our new bedroom."

But the dog wouldn't budge from the door.

"Come on now, there's no way I'm going to sleep on my own in a house with sixteen empty bedrooms... Rufus!"

Still the dog wouldn't budge. Even worse, he started whining.

Oh lord, there must be a ghost in here. Milly felt a tingle down her spine and the room felt eerily quiet.

"Oh, come on Rufus stop being so silly."

Still, he just stared straight ahead into the room with his tail between his legs, then did an about turn and raced away into the main part of the house.

"Look ghost, whoever you are, please, I am a nice lady. I'm sure we can get along quite nicely. Please don't freak me, my dog or my guests out. I have a living to make now you know."

That's all I need. A resident ghost wrecking everything.

"Rufus? Rufus? Where are you? Come here, you silly dog... There you are." He was in his dog basket, sadly chewing his toy. "Come on now," Milly bent down to pat him. "It's okay old boy. I know this must feel strange for you. It's strange for me too."

His tail started wagging feebly as he nuzzled Milly's hand.

"Don't you start going crazy on me, this is our new home."

She continued patting her old friend, studying him closely.

"We'll get used to it darling."

The ghost must have taken note because Milly managed to get the poor dog back into the bedroom, albeit with a treat. There was no doubt he was unsettled in that part of the house as he kept whining and looking around the rooms.

Poor old soul, maybe he missed their old home and was wondering where Jack was. He must think it strange he's sleeping in the same room as me.

After a lot of patting and coaxing he settled down to sleep on an old, folded blanket at the foot of Sophie's old bed. Milly hadn't slept in a single bed for over forty years.

It felt odd but not unpleasant. Easier than sleeping on her own in the bedroom she and Jack shared for so many years.

I'm so lucky that I could move on to somewhere new, she reflected, thinking of her friend Liz, who was so desperate to move after the death of her husband. But her friend just didn't have that option. There was no sweeping her memories into neat little boxes and starting afresh. Milly reflected as she switched off the light and tried to sleep. But every little creek or rattle made her frantically grapple for the light on the bedside table.

C'mon now, get a grip. she told herself, a house like this just had to have a resident ghost, nevertheless, Milly was quaking under her single sheets.

Jack, See 'em off. You need to protect your Missus...

***

Milly spent the next few days pottering about in the garden. It took a whole day to cut the grass and do some weeding. The pots at the front of the house looked a bit sad, so she bought some gorgeous scarlet, trailing petunias. Holly had left the tables and chairs in the cafe area at the back of the garden. Sitting down at one of the tables and surveying the garden, Milly reflected on the idea of opening up the café.

It's certainly the season for cream teas, but I'm not ready to put the sign back up yet... Even though I can bake, I need to get to grips with serving breakfasts and managing the rooms first. Of course, I could get someone in to help... Sophie is the obvious candidate. Oh, if only she'd leave London...

As much as she tried to hide it, even from herself, Milly was worried for her daughter. After Jack married Magda, Sophie dropped the idea of going to university, had a string of hopeless boyfriends and fell into a job that was leading nowhere.

I never realised she was still so bitter about everything. Was it our fault she lost her way?

Sophie and Jack had been so close. She was always his little Princess, and it broke Milly's heart when she referred to her once beloved father as 'a dirty old man'.

Just at that moment, a lovely little Robin landed on the table where Milly was sipping her coffee. He was unbelievably close and he stared at Milly with his tiny beady eyes, fluffing his little red chest and prancing on the spot. Milly was overtaken by a beautiful sense of peace and calm. Incredibly, he pecked a couple of crumbs of her croissant from her outstretched hand.

You've sent him, haven't you Jack? I feel your presence.

***

Chapter Four

It was around lunch-time when the door-bell rang and Rufus went berserk barking as Milly opened the door to her first guest, the actor Charlie Worsley.

"Hi there Mrs Henderson, I'm Charlie," he said extending his hand.

What a lovely lad. Milly took to him instantly. Shaking hands, she invited him in with his copious bags, introduced him to Rufus and showed him up to his room.

"Lovely house you have here."

"Thank you. I've just moved in. You are my first guest."

He clearly thought this was hysterically funny.

"So, you'll always remember me then?"

Milly wasn't quite sure what to make of that, but agreed that she was sure she would. After showing him the bathroom next to his room and discussing what time he wanted breakfast, Charlie said he was going to get his head down for a bit.

"I've got to be at the theatre by six to get into my costume and make up. The performance starts at eight every night. So, I usually have a couple of hours kip in the afternoon."

"Okay, that's fine. What do you usually do for supper?"

"Haven't thought of that. I'll probably grab a MacDonald's or something after the show."

Milly's mothering instincts immediately kicked in.

"Look, if you want to use my kitchen that's fine."

"Wow, that would be great Mrs Henderson. Do you have a microwave?"

Milly was polishing the copper kettles and irons around the large open fire-place in the dining room, when Rufus barked at the door.

Damn, that was a really good bit of 'Woman's Hour.'

"Afternoon Ma'am," a burly gentleman said as she opened the door, "I've come to pick up a Mr Charlie Worsley?"

Milly looked at her watch, it was a quarter to six.

"Okay, I'll give him a knock." Milly went upstairs to his room and knocked on his door. Silence. She knocked again, harder.

"Charlie! Your taxi's here..."

Suddenly the door opened revealing a very sleepy looking Charlie.

"Oh my God! What time is it? I overslept. Thanks, Mrs Henderson. Be down in a minute. Thank you. Thank you." he said rushing back into his room.

"But Charlie you haven't had anything to eat."

"No time now, I'll be fine really," he said, running back into his room and grabbing a bag. The next thing Milly knew he flew past her down the stairs, combing his hair as he went.

"Charlie?" Milly called after him, "You've got toothpaste round your mouth!"

Milly, being Milly, fretted all evening over the fact that the poor boy hadn't had anything proper to eat before he dashed off to his show. It really wasn't much fun cooking for one, so she made a nice risotto and put half aside for him. She'd leave a note on his door. He could pop it into the microwave when he got in.

It felt good having him in the house and Milly had stocked up on eggs, bacon and hash browns for his breakfast in the morning. She'd already laid his table and felt really excited about cooking for her first guest.

Switching off the lights in the dining room she made her way to bed. Miss James was arriving tomorrow, life was getting exciting at 'Willow Cottage.'

She was just drifting off to sleep when she heard a commotion outside. A woman was laughing and running down the gravel drive. Then the doorbell rang and Rufus was up and barking for all he was worth, desperate to get to the front door.

Crikey, its one in the morning! Who on earth is that?
Pulling on her dressing gown and slippers, Milly followed him out to the hall. Charlie was at the door looking harassed.

"Thanks, Mrs H. I'm really sorry, I forgot my key… No, sorry, you can't come in, glad you enjoyed the show." he called over to a vague female figure standing in the shadows. "Good night."

"Really sorry about that Mrs H. She waited for me after the show then followed me back here. Blimey, she must have been about forty."

"Occupational hazard eh?"

"Something like that."
He was far too charming to get cross with and seemed genuinely sorry to have got Milly up.

"Well, just remember your key next time."

"I will Mrs H, yes, really sorry to get you up."

"Are you hungry?"

"Starving."

"Well, there's some risotto in the fridge. Just pop it in the microwave."

"You're a star Mrs H."

***

"Charlie Worsley? He's really well-known mum. He played Max, in 'Wellington Square', Sophie commented on the phone the next morning.

"Ooh, so I've got a famous actor in the house?"

"You do, think I'll come down and check him out. Well, at least he didn't sneak anyone in. Groupies, you know what they're like?"

"He might have done if she'd been younger."

"Now stop mothering him Mum, he's a big boy. Just remember, you're in this business to make money, you can't be making meals for free."

"I know, don't worry, I'm sure we will come to some arrangement."

"So, you are going to cook for him every night?"

"I didn't say that dear."

Chapter Five

"Do you have a spare room I could book for my Dad, Mrs H? He always likes to see my shows. He'd like to come on Saturday night if that's okay?"

"I think we could fit him in," Milly answered as she served Charlie a couple of perfectly poached eggs. "Are you off to the gym now?"

"Yeah, got to work on my six-pack, you never know, I could be playing James Bond next."

"Okay, see you later," Milly smiled, clearing his plates away and giving Rufus a piece of uneaten toast.

"Right now, Miss James is coming this morning Rufus. Better get my skates on."

At Eleven o'clock, the doorbell rang on cue.

"Good morning, you must be Miss James? I'm Milly."
Wow, what an attractive lady she is.
Although she looked very old, she stood perfectly upright, was extremely smartly dressed and sported a very well-manicured set of bright-red fingernails. With her perfectly bobbed silver-grey hair, tinted with the slightest hint of violet, Milly thought she had to be an ex-actress.

"Good morning. Oh dear, please mind Fang," she said, looking daggers at Rufus and clutching her diminutive Chihuahua closer to her chest. "Holly always used to lock her dog away when we came… Ooh, Fang, don't worry darling!" she wailed as the animal starting yapping and snarling at Rufus, who looked totally perplexed.

"Okay, well we didn't know that, did we Rufus?" said Milly feeling distinctly annoyed as she put Rufus in the kitchen.

"Let me help you to your room… Hello Fang."
The dog immediately started snarling and snapped at Milly's fingers when she tried to stroke it.

"Fang, darling, everything is okay," cooed Miss James, "That big, horrid dog is safely locked away now."

Big horrid dog? Milly had to stop herself from saying something she regretted. *Remember now Milly, your guest must be at least 105.*

"Oh, dear this isn't my usual room."

"Oh, oh dear, which one do you normally have?" After a couple of minutes puzzling, the old lady said decisively, "The Lavender room."

"Er, well, this is the Lavender room."

"No, I've never been in this room before."

"Well, I only have one Lavender room."

"Oh well, it'll have to do, but it wasn't this one, I assure you," she said putting the dog down who immediately started snapping in circles around Milly's feet.

"My daughter should be here soon and Holly always used to bring us up some coffee and biscuits."

"Well, I can certainly get you some in the dining room."

"Oh no, I can't possibly leave Fang. That's why Holly always used to bring us our coffee up here."

A couple of minutes later, the doorbell rang.

Great saved by the bell.

"Hello, I'm Marcia, Maud's daughter. I hope she's behaving herself."

The polar opposite of her mother, Marcia was short and stocky, sporting a tweed suit, and a masculine haircut, her face devoid of any makeup.

"Oh yes, everything's fine. She's just arrived and is in her room. She said you usually have a coffee upstairs?"

"Oh, that's new to me. But yes, that would be lovely, thank you."

Oh no, now I've set a precedent.

"Have you met the irrepressible Fang?"

"Er, yes."

"Horrid little thing isn't it? Mother won't go anywhere without it."

After traipsing upstairs with coffee and biscuits and nearly getting her toes bitten off, Milly was alerted by Rufus to another knock on the door.

Foul, snappy little creature, Milly fumed, going down to answer it.

"Good morning, you must be Mrs Henderson? I'm Bill, Charlie's Dad."

Milly was momentarily lost for words. She hadn't seen such an attractive man in a very long time. Casually dressed in a denim shirt and black jeans, he had a great head of dark, greying shaggy hair, a neatly trimmed moustache and goatee beard and the darkest, brown, twinkly eyes. It was hard to put an age on him but Milly estimated he had to be in his fifties.

"Don't tell me, he's either fast asleep or in the gym?"

Milly felt herself blushing and it wasn't a hot flush.

For goodness sake, get a hold of yourself girl. You're a grieving widow.

"He left for the gym about fifteen minutes ago."

"Okay, I'll give him a call. Did he ask you if I could have a room for the next couple of nights? I always like to see his shows."

"Yes, that's fine," Milly gabbled, "Would you like to come up and see which one you'd like?"

"This'll do nicely," he said when Milly showed him into the 'Wallflower' room. "I hope my son is behaving himself..."

"Oh yes, it's a pleasure having him here, it really is. He was my first guest."

"So, this is a new venture for you?"

"It is, there wasn't a lot of money left in the pot after my husband died," *Oh no, why did I say that?* "So, I sold our house in London and decided to start afresh here."

"I am sorry for your loss," he said, as he studied Milly's face, "But good for you, it really is a wonderful house."

"Thank you, would you like a look around?"

"I'd like that very much. Where do we start?"

Milly felt a glow of excitement as he followed her through the house. He was very taken with the picture of Miss Gibbons and her raggedy children.

"Oh, how rude of me, I haven't offered you any coffee."

"Don't worry, I'll get one in town. Thank you anyway," he said holding her with his eyes for a moment. *What a pretty woman*, he could see why his son had been so complimentary about her. And her charming enthusiasm for the house was infectious.

***

"So, Charlie's Dad's staying? What's he like?" Sophie asked on the phone, later that night.

Milly found herself getting a bit girly and gigglish.

"Nice, very nice. Handsome too."

"Ooh, mum, you fancy him?"

"I didn't say that."

"You don't have to. Think you're turning into a bit of a merry widow!"

Chapter Six

"Right Mrs H. I've got complimentary tickets for you and my Dad to see my show tonight. Don't worry if you can't make it, they're comps, so I can get you one for another night."

"Oh Charlie, that's so sweet, thank you." Milly suddenly felt 'all of a jitter' at the prospect of going out with a man, "Of course, I'll come."

"Great, I'm going for a quick kip, my Dad'll drive you. Curtain up at 8.00pm. Oh, and don't worry about dinner, Dad and I had a big lunch."

Calm down now, a man as attractive as him is bound to have a girlfriend. Charlie had never mentioned his mother, so Milly presumed they weren't still together.

However, she was aware that she was going to a lot of time and effort getting ready that night. Couldn't look as if she had gone to too much effort though, so after a lot of chopping and changing her mind, Milly decided she would wear her 'French Connection' black trouser suit that Sophie always said she looked good in.

Yes, that and maybe my simple, coral coloured, silk top. A bit of eyeliner and blusher and amber coloured lipstick and voilà, I'm ready. Stepping back from the mirror she took in her reflection. *For goodness sake calm down. This isn't a date.*

The butterflies started fluttering again when Bill knocked on the dining room door.

"Shall we make a move then?" he asked, "Show starts at eight, so maybe we could get a quick drink in?"

"Sounds good to me," Milly answered, picking up her handbag. "See you later Rufus, be good. We, er, I, won't be long."

Bill smiled at her correcting herself.

"And may I say that you look very lovely tonight Mrs. Henderson."

"Oh, do call me Milly, thank you, well, I do scrub up well."

"Right now," Bill smiled, "What would you like to drink?" he asked, as they made their way into the bustling theatre bar.

"A gin and tonic would be lovely, thank you."

"Think I'll join you."

Oh, do stop looking at him, Milly chided herself, aware that she was peering at Bill over the top of her glass.

"It's always a relief when these shows have a good long run," Bill said, "Charlie gets very anxious in between shows."

"He has done very well by the sounds of it, seven years on 'Wellington Square,' that's pretty impressive."

"Yes, he loved it but didn't want to get too type-cast, so took the plunge and left. So far, he's had a good run, eighteen months in 'Flypast' then six months making a film and now 'Birdsong' for three months."

"Good for him," Milly said, "I think that is very brave. He was obviously quite well known when he was on television, a lot of young people wouldn't have wanted to give all that celebrity status up."

"True," Bill agreed, draining his drink and checking his watch. "Think we'd better go and get our seats."

It was a splendid performance. Charlie was the ultimate professional; completely transformed into a dashing young man during the first World War and despite his worries, he didn't fluff his lines once. Milly thought how proud his father must be of him. When the cast took their bow at the end of the show, Bill stood up and applauded. Milly wanted to do the same but thought better of it, after all, the rest of the cast might think she was Charlie's mother. And she didn't want to embarrass him or his father.

"What a wonderful performance, you must be so proud of your son," Milly said as Bill parked his BMW at 'Willow Cottage' after the performance. Charlie wasn't with them as he went out with the rest of the cast after the show.

"Yes, I am," Bill said, "He didn't have an easy start in life. His mum died of cancer when he was a year old, so he had a lot of different nannies throughout his life. But it made him very independent. He had to be, with me working all the time."

Milly was lost for words.

How terrible. Life could be so cruel. This young mother and son never really knew each other. They'd all missed out on so much.

Rufus came bounding up as soon as they were through the door.

"Well, thank you for a lovely evening. It was great to have some company tonight. 'Night Rufus, hope you weren't too lonely tonight." Bill said, giving him a quick rub behind his ears. "Night Milly."

"Good night Bill. Would you like a full English breakfast or a more continental start to the day?"

"Oh, it has to be a full English."

A crushing sense of loneliness overtook Milly as she watched him make his way up the stairs.

Milly didn't normally put her 'face' on first thing in the morning but with the arrival of Bill she had a definite spring in her step, which demanded she make a little more effort with her make-up and hair.

"Morning Mrs H," Charlie said brightly as he sat down for breakfast. Bill had come down a minute or so before him.

"Um, you are looking very well today," he said, studying her closely." Milly blushed to the soles of her feet.

"Thank you, Charlie."

He smiled at her knowingly, both knew that she'd been rumbled.

"May I say, you were quite brilliant last night Charlie, the power of make-up eh?" she joked, "You were so dashingly attractive, I hardly recognised you."

"Watch it now son, Milly might turn into a groupie," Bill said as he stirred his coffee.

"Speaking of groupies," Charlie laughed, "One followed me back the first night I was here, didn't she Mrs. H?"

They were all having a jolly good laugh about Charlie and his fan club when Miss James poked her head around the dining room door.

"Milly dear, my daughter is coming to pick me up in a few minutes, so can we settle the bill?"

"Yes, of course, Miss James."

"Thank you dear. Oh, oh, dearie me." she squealed as Fang suddenly leapt out of her handbag, did a couple of frenzied circuits around the dining room, under the startled gaze of Charlie and his father, then charged straight out of the front door, which someone had left ajar.

"Fang? Fang! Come back!" the old lady gasped, clutching her chest in horror.

"Don't worry we'll get him," Bill said gallantly "Come on Charlie get your skates on."

"Oh yes, sure," Charlie answered, running out the door after his father.
Milly was horrified.

"Don't worry Miss James, they will find him, I'm sure he won't have gone far." *Please Bill, please Charlie, find the horrid little thing,* Milly prayed fervently.

"It's okay, we've got him" an out of breath Bill proclaimed as he came through the front door clutching Fang. It could only have been less than ten minutes or so since they'd gone, but it felt like an eternity.

"There you go, he didn't go far, we found him hiding under Milly's car."

"Oh, thank you, thank you both so much. Fang darling," she cried, nearly asphyxiating the dog with her cuddles.

"Hello, may I come in?" Miss James' daughter's, jolly hockey-stick voice called from the hallway.

"Oh, Marcia, I nearly lost Fang, he ran out the door."

"Hmph, that's a pity," her daughter whispered surreptitiously to a very relieved Milly. "Ah well, that's good Mother, no harm done then. All's well that ends well. Come along now, we really have to hit the road. Have you settled up with Mrs Henderson?"

"No dear, I was just about to when Fang shot out of the house."

"Thank you so much for having Mother, Marcia said to Milly, pulling out a bundle of notes from a tatty leather purse. I've put in a little extra from Fang."

"That's so sweet, it really isn't necessary."

"Ah, but it is. It's not many landladies who would welcome such a snappy little guest."
Just as they were disappearing through the door, Miss James turned to Charlie.

"Here dear," she said giving him a fifty-pence coin, "Buy yourself some sweets."
Luckily, Charlie caught on quickly and put on a splendid impromptu performance.

"Thank you very much, that's very kind of you. I'll buy myself a comic."

"Blimey, I didn't know I looked that young," he whispered, to his father and Milly, who were desperately trying to suppress their giggles.

"Oh, my goodness, thank God she's gone," Milly said, giving full reign to her laughter and sinking into the nearest chair.

"Thank you both so much, I don't know what I would have done without you. I thought Miss James was about to have an apoplectic fit."

"So, did I," Bill agreed, laughing as much as Milly.

"Right, I'm off to the gym," Charlie smiled, ruffling his hair, "Just thought, do you think they'll let me in? Better take my ID!"

"Okay, shall we meet somewhere for a quick lunch?" Bill suggested, still laughing.

"Only if you're paying…"

"He's serious you know," Bill winked at Milly.
This was the first time Milly had a really good belly laugh since Jack died. Stupidly she felt guilty.

**

"Thank you so much Milly," Bill said, as he settled his bill the next day. It's a great comfort to me knowing that Charlie has found himself such a lovely place to stay. You know how it is, however old they are, you never stop worrying?"

"I know," Milly answered, give me a bunch of five-year-old's any day. I'm always worrying about my daughter. It's lovely for me, having Charlie here, and you are welcome any time." Milly thought she would melt, when he handed her back the keys to his room, holding her in his gaze with those twinkly eyes.

"Just thought," he asked as he was half way out the door, "Do you have a couple of rooms next weekend maybe?"

I knew he had a girlfriend.

Chapter Seven

"Great, Mum, better go. My boss is on the prowl. I'll call you when the train is approaching Chichester." Milly was so excited. Sophie had taken the week off and was bringing Zac down for his half-term holiday. Of course, Magda was more than happy. Wanting them both to feel at home, Milly rushed out and bought a 'Ninja Turtles' duvet set for whichever bed Zac chose to sleep in and a nice vanilla scented candle for Sophie's room. She also stocked up on kiddy-type snacks and drinks and checked out all the local child-friendly entertainment. *I know he'll bring his playstation down but we must get him out into the fields,* Milly mused over her ironing. *I want to see him throw a few sticks for Rufus and jump in some puddles like Ben and Jake used to do at his age... Must make sure that Magda packs some old clothes and wellies.*

But Milly knew that Magda wouldn't remember and would make a terrible to-do if his designer clothes and trainers got muddy. So she bought him an inexpensive tracksuit and a pair of cheap trainers for him to muck about in at 'Willow Cottage'.

The next day, she was waiting on the platform for their train.

"Nana!" Zac shouted running into her arms, leaving Sophie to struggle with all his bags.

Milly could have cried, she didn't realise how much she had missed him, and of course it was wonderful that Sophie was here too.

"My God Mum, the train took ages. Talk about the scenic route. We could have flown to Italy and back."

"Oh darling, that's not what you need with a rambunctious little boy. Was he okay on the train?"

"So-so," Sophie raised her eyebrows, "Luckily he had his Gameboy, then I let him play on my phone."

As Milly expected Zac was over-awed by the size of the house.

"There's so many rooms Nana."

"Yes, there are darling."

"Where do you sleep?"

"I sleep in here."

"Where will I sleep?"

"You can have a room on your own or sleep with Sophie or Rufus and me."

The little boy thought for a moment, torn between choosing Milly or Sophie.

"I'll sleep with Auntie Sophie Nana, because you have Rufus, looking after you."

"Okay, darling that's fine. Do you want to phone your Mum and tell her that you are here?"

"Nah," he said running off into the garden.

"Magda's not bothered Mum. She didn't even come to the door, just sent him off with all his stuff. No goodbyes or anything."

Milly rolled her eyes.

"Best not fall out with her. She could stop us seeing Zac." Milly said, giving Sophie a cup of tea as they sat down at the kitchen table.

"That won't ever happen. She can't off-load her son quick enough. I've got some news for you Mum. You might need a gin and tonic."

"It's a bit early isn't it dear?"

"Well, let's just pretend its seven o'clock".

Feeling apprehensive, Milly fetched the gin.

"Go on then, spill the beans."

Sophie took a deep breath.

"I'm pregnant.

Milly stopped pouring the gin, mid-flow and fixed her daughter with a shocked stare.

"I know you never liked Lloyd," Sophie gabbled nervously, "But we're going to try and make a go of it."

It was true. Milly never liked Lloyd. '*A weasely, little man,*' as Jack referred to him, who did '*something*' in the music business and had a fondness for the '*white powder.*' Sophie was always having to cough-up his share of the rent and they never had any money to go on holiday like all their other friends. Sophie was always making excuses about why 'they couldn't do this or that'.

"But Soph, I thought you weren't together anymore?"

"Well, no, we weren't…"

"So, you are 'together' now? Are you happy?"

"Yes, Mum, *we're* happy," Sophie, pointedly answered.

"Where will you live?"

"The flat of course."

"Oh," Milly remarked. *Surely, they aren't going to take a baby back to that awful, place?*

"Mum, we'll be fine. Don't worry. Lloyd's going to do the place up. Aren't you happy for me? This will be your first grandchild?"

For the sake of her daughter, Milly tried to sound more enthusiastic.

"Yes, of course I am darling… You could always live here? There's plenty of room."

"It wouldn't work with Lloyd's schedule Mum. He always has to go out to gigs and they're usually in London. But thank you so much for the offer."

"It's a shame Lloyd couldn't come down and share this announcement."

Sophie started tripping over her words, saying something about how '*Lloyd wanted to be there but work took over.*'

Milly wanted to run upstairs and hide away in one of the rooms and cry but knew she couldn't.

Oh God, why did the father have to be him?

Despite the shock news of her impending grand-motherly status, they had a lovely week, and Milly was reassured that come what may, Sophie was happy and would make a wonderful mother. There was no doubting that she had a great way with Zac, and happily kept him entertained all week with trips to the swimming pool, cinema and trampolining park. Milly couldn't have coped without her.

Shortly before they were due to get the train back to London, they both came in looking a little sheepish. Zac was carrying something that looked like it was wrapped up in a tea cosy.

"It's for you Nana."

"Sorry Mum, we just couldn't resist."

Milly couldn't believe her eyes. It was a tiny, black, pot-bellied piglet.

"A breeder is selling them locally and well, we just thought you'd love one."

"Sophie, I know you are getting all maternal but my mothering days are over."

"Oh no, are you cross?"

It was adorable with its tiny, twitching snout.

"Do you like him Nana?"

"He is rather sweet... What shall we call him?"

"Dad."

"Dad?"

"Yes, 'Dad'." The little boy answered, his eyes filling with tears. "I want your piggy to be called 'Dad', Nana."

***

Before Milly knew it, it was the weekend. Bill was due to arrive with Charlie's grandmother the next day. *Whoopee! So, he wasn't coming with some glamorous girlfriend.* Milly's eyes lit up when Charlie told her. She just hoped it wasn't obvious that she was so relieved. Sophie and Zac had gone back to London and Milly had to admit, her little, snouty friend helped to fill the void. Even Rufus was quite taken with the little fella and took to putting his head on Milly's lap when she was feeding him.

"Hey Charlie, come and see my new resident guest." Milly said, leading him into the ironing room when he came in from his show. Although desperate to go to bed, she had to stay up and give her new 'baby' his night feed.

"This sounds interesting Mrs H… What have we here?" He asked, peering into the box where 'Dad' was snoozing.

"It's a pig?"

"Yes."

"It isn't going to end up on my plate is it? I've heard of going organic but…"

"Certainly not, here, do you fancy feeding him?" Milly said giving him a bottle of milk.

"Er... yeah."

"Go on then, pick him up."

"Um, do you want to hand *it* to me?" Milly placed the wriggling bundle in Charlie's arms.

"Hold the bottle up, make sure the teat is in his mouth… yes, that's right… much better."
Charlie didn't look convinced but thought he'd better persevere. As the pig latched on the bottle he looked more at ease.

"This is quite relaxing Mrs H. Just what I need to come down after a show. What's his name?"

"Dad."

"Dad?"

"It's a long story."

"Dad and Grandma will love this," he laughed. "A pig called 'Dad.' "

"Yes, it is quite funny. So, your Grandma's coming tomorrow?"

"Yeah, she likes to see my shows." He said putting down 'Dad's empty bottle. "Typical if I go and fluff my lines. It's always the way when all your friends and family are there. Well, I quite enjoyed that. 'Dad' and I have now bonded," he said handing him back to Milly.

"Careful. I'll put you on night-duty next."

Around five o'clock the following afternoon, Bill arrived with Charlie's grandmother. Milly's heart missed a beat as she saw him standing on the doorstep, through the glass panel of the front door. Their eyes held each other for a moment as she opened the door. Dressed in his signature black jeans and a grey linen shirt he looked as deliciously handsome as ever.

"This is Norah, Milly. Charlie's grandmother."

"Hello there," Milly said extending her hand, "Lovely to meet you, come in."

Small and plump, with tightly permed, grey hair, Norah's face broke into an easy smile.

"Oh, what a lovely house you have. Charlie told me all about it. He also said you have a baby pig."

"Yes, courtesy of my daughter."

"How lovely."

"Let me show you your room," Milly went to take Norah's cases but Charlie gallantly insisted on carrying them for his grandmother.

"Oh, my goodness, all the rooms are named after flowers," Norah commented.

"Yes, I think they've always been named after flowers, the plaques look pretty ancient. I've no plans to change them."

"That's good," Norah smiled putting her pretty little pink vanity case on the bed.

Milly showed her how to work the television and pointed out where the kettle, coffee and tea were in the room.

"Now just one more very important thing. What would you like for breakfast?"

"So how was the show?" Milly asked Norah the next morning when she came down for breakfast.

"Wonderful, just wonderful." Norah answered, "It always amazes me how our Charlie remembers his lines. He was never like that with his times-tables at school," she said, smiling at the memory.

"You must be so proud when you see him on stage," Milly commented as she put a pot of tea on the table.

"Yes, I am," Norah remarked sadly. "I just wish my daughter could see him now. Ah, Janey…" she sighed sadly.

"Tell me about the last show Charlie was in?" Milly asked softly.

"Oh, his last show? Yes, that was wonderful too, it was 'Flypast' - all about the RAF pilots in the Second World war. Charlie played one of the young pilots. It was incredible how knowledgeable he became about the war. The director arranged for a lot of veterans to talk to all the actors about their experiences. It was such a shame his grandfather never got to see it, he'd been in the RAF too."

"Hey, Grandma," Charlie said, coming into the dining room and kissing the old lady on the cheek, "You haven't been telling Milly about how I dropped my drinks tray down the leading lady's dress in that one have you?"

"Ooh, I forgot about that, that was the best bit." Norah joked, then told Milly all about it.

"Dad said he'd give breakfast a miss Mrs H, he's not feeling too bright this morning."

"Your actor friends did keep topping up his glass," Norah remarked, tucking into her scrambled eggs.

"Shall I take him up something?" Milly asked, concerned.

"No, he'll be fine, thanks anyway. Right now, Grandma, you said you wanted to have a walk across those fields. Shall we take Rufus Mrs H?"

"Yes, that would be great, Charlie, thank you."

Bill came down later in the morning and went straight out with Charlie and Norah for some lunch. Even though he was his usual, charming, handsome self, Milly noticed that he did look a bit on the pale side. But he drove Norah home to Guildford that afternoon and said he'd pop in to see Charlie off to his performance before headed back to London.

"No sign of my Dad Mrs H? Thought he'd be back from dropping Grandma off by now," Charlie asked when he came down from his pre-show sleep.

"Maybe something came up and he had to go straight home," Milly remarked, surprised that Bill would just take off like that.

"Yeah, that makes sense," Charlie said, I can't hang around for him though," he said checking his watch. "If he turns up, can you tell him I had to go?"

He didn't turn up and Milly started to worry. Supposing some-thing had happened to him? She didn't really know him, but she didn't think he would tell Charlie he was coming back if he wasn't. On the other hand, he had settled his tab so he didn't really have to come back. *Oh, do stop fretting,* Milly told herself. *Go and do some ironing.*

***

The landline rang just as she was making a nice, wholesome, pea and ham soup.

"Hello, a kindly female voice said, "We have been trying to contact Mr Charlie Worsley whom we believe is staying with you."

"Yes, he is." Milly answered, trying to sound calm.

"We have been trying to call him but can't get through to him on his phone. Is he there?"

"No, he's performing at the Festival Theatre and won't be back until later tonight. Can I help at all? I run 'Willow Cottage' and will be seeing him later tonight. Shall I ask him to call you?"

The woman was quiet for a moment.

"I'm the Sister in the Cardiology wing at St. Richard's Hospital in Chichester, I am afraid his father has had a heart attack."

Milly felt as though she'd had a sudden blow to her head.

"Oh, my goodness, Is he okay?" A sick feeling crept into her stomach.

"Yes, he is conscious and talking. He admitted himself a few hours ago, complaining of pains in his arm and chest. He wanted to check if he was okay to drive home.

"We did various tests and discovered he had a heart attack earlier today."

"So, he didn't collapse?"

"No, luckily he was sensible enough to admit himself."

"Thank goodness for that." Milly switched into efficient, practical mode. "I can collect his son straight after the show and drive him to the hospital. Should be around 10.30, if that's okay?"

"Yes, that's fine, his son will be able to see him. Mr Worsley's in the Cardiology Ward, on the ground floor. Milly wanted to cry. Poor, poor Bill.

And now she had to tell Charlie.

***

"Hey, Mrs H, what are you doing here?" Charlie asked as he filed through the stage door with the rest of the cast.

There was no point in mincing her words.

"Everything is okay Charlie, but the hospital phoned about half an hour ago to say that your Dad has been admitted to the Cardiology ward. He had a heart attack earlier today."

The colour drained from the boy's face as he stood stock-still, digesting the news.

"Hey Charlie, you coming to the pub mate?" one of the actors asked.

"No, not tonight Hugh," Charlie answered, looking straight ahead.

"I'll take you to the hospital," Milly said calmly "They said your Dad is conscious, sitting up and talking normally."

Charlie looked dumbfounded and followed Milly mutely to her car.

"Try not to worry Charlie, he is in the best place."

They walked into the hospital and Milly escorted him to the nurse's station on the Cardiology Ward.

"Okay, now you go in. There are phones direct to the taxi rank in the reception by the lifts. You don't even have to pay for the call. Go on now, go in. Your Dad will want to see you."

"Thanks, Mrs. H…" The boy had tears in his eyes. "He will be okay, won't he?"

"Of course, he will Charlie, he'll be fine."

Milly walked back to the car in a daze.

That poor, poor boy. And Bill. He had to be okay.

She couldn't settle to anything when she got home. Thank goodness for Rufus, who seemed to tune into everything Milly was feeling and it was nice to have the diversion of 'Dad'.

About an hour or so later Milly heard Charlie come through the front door.

"Charlie," she leapt up from the sofa, "How is your father?"

"Alright," Charlie answered in a monotone. "He was awake and quite chatty. He said he had just driven back from Grandma's house when he felt a crushing weight across his back which travelled down his arm. So, he checked himself into the A&E at the hospital. The pains were getting worse and travelling up into his jaw. A blood test showed that he'd had a heart attack. I can't believe it Mrs H. My Dad, having a heart attack? I thought people keeled over."

"Me too Charlie, it just goes to show. Well, look on the bright side, he didn't collapse, and from what you say, he is quite chirpy."

"He looks perfectly normal and he kept saying he can't believe this has happened. Then he kept apologising to me, saying he was sorry. He doesn't want me to tell Grandma because it will worry her... Oh Mrs H, why did he keep apologising to me?"

And with that the boy broke down.

Milly held him in her arms and let him cry.

After he had recovered himself a little, Charlie told Milly that his father would be having an angiogram the next day to assess the damage to his heart. The worst-case scenario was that he would have to have some type of bypass operation, or it could mean something as simple and straight-forward as a stent, which Charlie explained, was like a tiny spring, inserted into a blocked artery to keep it open. The nurse had given him a brochure which explained the procedure.

Milly was hoping against hope that Bill just needed a stent.

Chapter Eight

Charlie went to see his father the next morning. He was distinctly subdued when he left the house and hadn't wanted any breakfast.

That poor boy doesn't know if he's coming or going, Milly sighed as she aimlessly flicked a duster in the dining room. Try as she might to settle to the diversion of the dusting, she couldn't help worrying.

Later that afternoon, the landline rang. To her utter amazement, it was Bill sounding bright and breezy. Milly felt a thrill of excitement when she heard his voice.

"Oh, Bill, how are you? I can't believe this has happened.

"I know, neither can I," he managed to laugh. "Well at least it didn't happen during Charlie's show. He would have had a hard job living that one down... Look Milly," he added in a more serious tone, "I just wanted to thank you for looking after Charlie. It's all been a bit of a shock for us both but I'm still alive and kicking. They are going to transfer me to Worthing hospital as soon as there is a bed because they have better facilities there."

"Is there anything I can do?"

"Keep an eye on my boy, please, and tell him to do his show tonight. I'm in the best possible place. 'The show must go on' as they say... and besides, his agent told him a film scout will be in the audience tonight. On no account must he miss that because of me."

"Okay, anything else?"

"You can come and tell me all about the latest antics at 'Willow Cottage', if you have the time. Quite an entertaining place you have there. Just check I'm still here and that they haven't transferred me first."

"Of course I will Bill," Milly said a little too enthusiastically. "See you later."

"He wants me to go and visit him Rufus!" Milly beamed as she put down her phone. "He wants me to go and see him!" she sang out loud as she did a little jig around the dining room and primped her hair in the mirror in the hall.

Rufus looked at his mistress quizzically. Not sure what to make of it all.

"Charlie!" Milly knocked on his door about an hour before he was due to go to the theatre. "I've brought you a snack."

A few seconds later Charlie rustled to the door, looking bleary eyed.

"Fab, Mrs H, you needn't have brought it up."

"Well, your Dad rang me and said he'd be really upset if you didn't go to the theatre tonight."

"I know… but…," he started to protest, ruffling his hair with his hand nervously. "I don't want him to be a 'Billy no mates' at visiting time. You know, with all the other patients surrounded by their families bearing bunches of grapes."

"Your Dad said he'd be very upset if that film scout missed your show-stopping performance tonight…" Charlie shuffled his feet…

"Look, I'd really like to pop in and see him tonight if that's all right with you?"

"Oh, that would be great Mrs H. I'm sure he'd like that very much." Charlie said, visibly brightening.

"Right then, that's settled. If I don't see you, there's fish pie in the fridge for when you come in."

"You're a star Mrs H, thanks a million."

"Now go and impress that film scout."

***

Bill was sitting up in bed looking nothing like Milly expected. Although he was covered with an assortment of coloured wires which hooked up to a bleeping and flashing monitor, he was as handsome, alert and chatty as ever.

His eyes lit up when he saw her.

"Hey Milly, thanks for coming in. How are you?"

"Never mind how I am, how are you?"

"A bit shocked but otherwise okay. I had an angiogram this morning which showed that I've got one blocked artery which they are going to unblock and keep open with one of these amazing little 'Stent' things," he said, passing her a pamphlet which fully illustrated the procedure. "They're transferring me to Worthing in the morning. Incredible, what they can do. It's all very quick, only about forty minutes and I can watch the whole procedure on the silver screen."

Those dark twinkly eyes were sending delicious shivers down Milly's spine.

"Milly?... There's something I need to ask you."

"Go ahead," Milly gulped.

"I've got to have complete bed rest for two weeks following the procedure. Charlie said he would look after me as he is around in the day, so I wondered if I could book a room with you for the next couple of weeks?"

"Of course, Bill, no problem at all."

"Thank you, that would be wonderful. I don't want to worry Norah. You are a very good woman, Milly." he added, touching her hand.

A tingle ran up Milly's spine. It was a very long time since anyone had made her feel like this.

"Now tell me about your guests. Any more dramas with escaping dogs?"

"No, thank goodness. I've got a crowd coming for the racing at Goodwood. They'll be staying all next week. I've inherited them from my predecessor."

They were just discussing the upcoming events and racing at Goodwood when a nurse came in.

"Hello, I've just got to check the incision where the catheter went in, it's okay Mrs Worsley, you needn't go on account of me," she said, suddenly pulling back the bed sheet and revealing Bill in all his glory. "Ah, yes, every-thing looks just fine." she said, prodding around his groin.

"Ah good," Milly gabbled, trying to hide her embarrassment as she scrabbled around for her handbag and jacket.

"See you later Bill, I'd better go and get my guests' bedrooms ready."

"Thanks for coming Milly," Bill winked, suppressing a smile.

Her cheeks were still burning when she got to her car. *The nurse thought I was his wife! Lord, how embarrassing but actually, how nice. How do we look as a couple?* She wondered, absent-mindedly buckling up her seat-belt. She giggled as she remembered the nurse whipping back Bill's bed sheet. There was no doubt that he was very well endowed below.

'*Nothing wrong with his wedding tackle*' as Milly's friend Margot would say. *Come to think of it, Bill looked in much better shape than Jack ever did.* Not that Milly was ever interested in the physical side of their marriage once she hit the menopause. All those night sweats and throwing off the bed-sheets hardly helped. So, when things went pear-shaped with Magda and Milly took Jack back, they tried watching a little porn to spice things up a bit but it was all so ridiculous they just ended up laughing. It was even more hilarious hiding all the films away in case the cleaner found them. Two sixty-year old's watching porn? You had to see the funny side even though Margot said it worked for her and Benny.

Right, this won't do! You've got guests coming, Milly reminded herself. But still she couldn't shake the memory of Bill in all his glory.

Move over Jack you've got competition.

Chapter Nine

Around eleven o'clock the next morning, a vintage Jaguar and immaculate Rolls Royce purred their way down the drive.

"Good morning, you must be the new owner?" A very dapper man who looked to be in his seventies, extended his hand. "I am Ernest Jackson and this is my wife Dorothy," he said, introducing a very pleasant looking lady, who looked remarkably un-lined for her age but had that tell-tale 'startled look' people sometimes get when they have overdone the Botox.

A minute or so later, an attractive youngish couple, who turned out to be their son and his wife, joined them at the front door.

Mother and daughter-in-law were armed with vintage hats and dresses on hangers, for the famous annual, three day 'Goodwood Revival' meeting. Evidently, this was going to be a very grand, delightfully British affair as race-goers from all over the country dress-up in a dazzling array of costumes, from the glamour of the roaring twenties to the nostalgic forties, fabulous fifties and swinging sixties. And this delightful family were going to make sure they arrived in style, hence the beautiful Jaguar and Rolls Royce now parked safely in Milly's drive.

"You should have seen the wonderful motor cars we passed travelling down here!" Ernest rubbed his hands in glee. "Hundreds of them weren't there darling? All 'Revival' race-goers like us, driving their beauties."

"Yes, it's a spectacular event," his wife readily agreed, "Goodwood will be crammed with rare and wonderful classic cars people are just dying to show off."

"It sounds wonderful, I hope you have a fabulous time," Milly said, helping them with their cases up the stairs to their rooms.

"It's great that you've got a dog." Mr Jackson said, making a fuss of Rufus, when they came back downstairs.

"Yes, the place wouldn't be the same without one," his wife added. "Holly used to let us take her dog Tess, with us for a walk across the fields. Might we be able to take your dog?" she asked hopefully, patting Rufus.

"Yes, of course," Milly said as she went to get his lead." He's very obedient and fine with other dogs."

"We were so pleased when Holly got married to that handsome racing driver," Mrs Jackson gushed. "He was a guest here you know. That's how they met. So, how are you settling in?"

"I'm still finding my feet as they say, but yes, so far so good," Milly smiled.

"Well, you will be seeing a lot more of us, we come every year. Did Holly book us in for 'Glorious Goodwood,' next month?"

"Yes, she did," Milly confirmed, checking her diary.

"Oh goody, 'Ladies Day,' is the highlight of my year. You should see the hats."

"Mum could hardly get in the car last year, her hat was so big," their son joked.

"I bet you looked gorgeous. You are all very welcome, I hope you have a fabulous time," Milly added, warmly as she clipped Rufus' lead to his collar.

Just as they were disappearing through the door to the fields, a rather stressed looking, young woman poked her head around the front door.

"Hello there, do you have a single room for the next couple of nights?"

"Yes, I do, would you like to come and have a look?"

"Oh great, that's a relief. No, whatever you have is fine, everywhere is booked because of Goodwood, I left it to the last moment, should have known..."

"So, are you a racing enthusiast?" Milly asked as she helped the young woman up the stairs with her bags.

"No, no... I'm an actor, I get paid to dress up and run around and look important along with about a hundred others actors at Goodwood. It's all great fun," she said kicking off her shoes and lying on the bed. "Gosh, it's such a relief you have a spare room. Don't know what I would have done otherwise!"

"Well, you are very welcome," Milly said, "If you could just sign in the Visitor's Book in the hall that would be great. One of my other guests is an actor too, he's performing in 'Birdsong' at the Chichester Theatre."

"Oh, that's interesting," she said, her eyes lighting up. "Would you mind if I order a pizza?" she asked hopefully, not sure if that would be allowed.

"Go ahead, Milly answered, what time would you like breakfast?"

"I've got an early start, so would around seven be okay?"

"That's fine," said Milly, not thinking it was fine at all. She distinctly remembered her predecessor saying she never served breakfast before eight.

"Full English, poached eggs on toast, kedgeree, kippers or scrambled eggs?"

"Ooh, a boiled egg would be great."

Damn, boiled eggs are the worst. You never know how people really liked them.

So that was settled. After giving her a set of keys, Milly reminded her where the dining room was, and left her to it. *What a pretty girl - and an actress too. I wonder if 'Willow Cottage' will weave its magic between her and Charlie...*

"Your Dad seemed fine," Milly said as Charlie came in from his evening performance later that night. "He's being transferred to Worthing Hospital tomorrow morning as they have better facilities there."

"That's good," Charlie answered, looking tired.

"You're early tonight."

"Yes, well, it didn't seem right, me going out with the cast when my Dad's in a hospital bed."

"He'll be fine Charlie, try not to worry too much. Now how about that fish pie?"

"Thanks, Mrs H, but I think I will have it tomorrow before the show if that's okay. Think I'll have an early night," he said, making his way towards the stairs.

"Okay, that's fine. How did it go with the scout by the way?"

"Wasn't my best performance but it wasn't my worst."

"I bet you did brilliantly. 'Night, Charlie."

"See you tomorrow Mrs H," he said, giving her a resigned smile.

Milly's heart ached for him.

***

"Oh, my goodness… you look wonderful," Milly exclaimed as Ciara, her resident actress, swept into the dining room the next morning.

"Thank you, it's taken me ages to do my hair," she laughed taking a seat at the little table laid for one, by the window.

Dressed as an Audrey Hepburn look-alike, she looked fantastic, with her perfectly coiffed hair, pearl choker, fifties style little black dress with the tiny nipped-in waist and billowing skirt.

"Well, last year I was a charlady, so this is a lot better," Ciara joked as she removed her long, black elbow-length gloves.

Milly had just given Ciara her boiled egg and rack of neatly cut toast when Charlie shuffled into the dining room. He was just going to have a quick bite of toast before going to the hospital to accompany his father in the ambulance to Worthing. His eyes nearly popped out of his head when he saw the beautiful Ciara.

"I don't usually dress like this," she smiled softly, in between lady-like bites of toast.

"This is Charlie," Milly said brightly, as she gave him his toast. Charlie looked completely over-awed by the lovely vision and just about managed to mumble hello.

"So, you are the actor Mrs Henderson mentioned? I hear you are in Birdsong."

"Yes, I am."

"I'm an actor too."

"Ah, that explains the costume. You're starting work early today."

"Yes, well, I just have to rush around and look busy at Goodwood. It's a nice little earner for us actors. I do it every year. Ah, great, my taxi's here," she announced checking her phone. "Maybe catch you later," she smiled, happily, swishing out the door.

Charlie was too captivated by her charms to answer.

Just as she was leaving, the Jackson entourage graced the dining room with their entrance.

Mrs Jackson was dressed in the most gorgeous, bright pink 1920's flapper dress, Charleston heels, white feather boa, black headband and long string of pearls, while her husband sported a tweed jacket, plus fours and a flat cap. Their son and his wife were dressed as a 1920's gangster and his moll.

Milly grabbed her camera.

"May I take a picture of you all?"

"Of course," Mrs Jackson replied, linking arms with her husband and encouraging their son and daughter-in-law to stand next to them as Milly snapped away happily.

"You'll be the first to grace my pin board," she announced excitedly.

Her breakfast went down a storm and Milly felt a real thrill as she watched those fabulous motor cars slowly crunch down her drive. All her guests that morning had perfectly captured that golden era of motor car racing. And just as Mr Jackson gave her a cheery toot, Milly heard the nostalgic drone of a low-flying Lancaster bomber, circling the skies above 'Willow Cottage'. Moments later it was joined by a Spitfire.

No doubt it was going to be a glorious day at Goodwood.

Chapter Ten

Charlie came back with Bill two days after his operation. Milly had offered to collect them but Bill was insistent that they'd get a taxi.

"Hello there Milly," Bill said brightly as he came into the hall. He looked fine although he was walking in slow, hesitant steps. Charlie, hovering nervously by his father's side, carried his bag.

"How are you feeling?"

"Like a new man," his eyes twinkled. "I don't like hospitals, it's good to be out."

Charlie was fretting, obviously concerned as they were about to negotiate the stairs to his room,

"C'mon now Dad, take it easy, hold on to me."

"Okay son, I'm fine."

"Just hold on to me Dad, I don't want you falling down the stairs."

Milly didn't want Rufus jumping up at Bill as soon as he came in the house so she shut him out in the garden when she heard the taxi in the drive. Once Bill was safely up-stairs in his room, she called the protesting Rufus back into the house.

Charlie seemed to have everything under control and Milly didn't want to intrude, but she'd made a nice ginger cake that morning that was just begging to be eaten.

Maybe they'd like some with a cup of tea. Yes, I'll just take some up on a tray and leave them to it.

Knocking softly on Bill's door, she took it in. Bill was tucked up in bed with Charlie sitting anxiously by his side.

"Just what the doctor ordered, thank you Milly," Bill smiled, weakly.

"Thank you, Mrs H," Charlie added, quietly.

There was a slightly tense atmosphere in the room and Milly was mindful not to intrude in to their privacy.

"Good to have you back, if there is anything you need, just ask…"

"Thanks, Mrs H," Charlie said softly as she left the room.

That poor boy. He looks totally shell-shocked.

"C'mon, Rufus, let's go and chase some rabbits," Milly remarked flatly, taking down his lead from its usual hook on the wall.

As they returned from their walk, she saw Charlie walking back from the village shop with a copy of 'The Times' for Bill.

"Hey there Mrs H, Rufus," he said more brightly.

"Hello Charlie, how's the patient?"

"So far, so good, he's not supposed to come down stairs for a week."

"You're going to have your work cut out. Make sure you get some rest before the show."

"Yeah, I will. Oh damn! I forgot his tea bags. He's been advised to cut back on caffeine and doesn't want to drink any coffee for the next few weeks so he's having Earl Grey tea instead…Right," he said turning, to walk back to the shop, "Can I get you anything?"

"I've got some Earl Grey tea bags he can have."

"Are you sure?"

"Of course, Charlie, it's just some tea bags," Milly said, as they made their way into the house.

"Here, take them up, with my compliments."

Bill was reading the paper when Milly knocked on the door with a pot of Earl Grey tea and more ginger cake later that afternoon.

"Room service!" She said, with a smile.

"Milly this is wonderful, thank you," Bill said, inviting her to sit on the bed.

"How are you?"

"I'm okay, Charlie is tending to my every need, I've got my paper and my laptop. It's just odd having to consciously slow down."

"That's just for now, you will be getting stronger, every day."

"I know, it's a shock suddenly being on so many pills," he said in a flat tone, indicating the mini-pharmacy on his bedside table.

"Well," Milly said brightly, "Thank God for them."

"Yes, thank God for them, My little champions! Don't think I'd last long without them. Now," he said, savouring his tea, "Enough about me, tell me about you, Milly. You said you lost your husband quite recently. I remember what it was like when I lost my Janey. But time is a great healer, as they say. So, how are you coping with it all?" Milly's eyes welled with tears, she just couldn't help herself. When anyone asked how she really was in a genuinely caring way, the flood gates opened.

"Sorry Bill," she said sniffling, "This is so embarrassing."

"My dear girl, of course it isn't. There's nothing more therapeutic than shedding a few tears. I know, I was always blubbering - at work, on the train, and once, suddenly in a shop. I know what it's like to lose someone, I've been there…"

And so it all came tumbling out. Milly told him everything about Jack, Magda, little Zac and why she had to make a living for the first time in her life when she had just turned sixty.
He took it all in.

"Men can be so silly, throwing away a good marriage for one stupid fling that ruins everything. I think we go through some kind of male menopause you know. He was lucky that you were so forgiving. Not many women would have taken him back."

"I know, I lost friends over it."

"Well, I bet he regretted it. Were you able to get over it? As a couple I mean?"

"It was hard. Every time we had a row the accusations and recriminations all came back with a vengeance. We went to counselling, and they said that for the marriage to work I'd have to stop bringing it up all the time. The kids were still at home and I knew I had to keep a lid on things, so for their sakes I did, and things got better." Milly said, shifting on the bed. She had inched closer to Bill's legs and it felt a bit intimate.

"As hard as it was for me," she continued, "It was just as difficult for Jack. The kids hardly looked at him the first year he was at home and of course Magda started to drain us financially. But the one great thing to come out of this was Zac. That little boy saved out marriage and our family."

Bill couldn't take his eyes off Milly.

What a selfless woman. Accepting another woman's child into the bosom of her family.

"So here you are starting again?"

"Yes, here I am."

"It takes time Milly; the pain never goes away, but you learn to live with it. You'd built up a life together."

"Yes, I suppose we did." Milly sniffed.

"That's something to be proud of. Janey died just as our life together was really starting."

"What happened?" Milly asked tentatively.

"Brain tumor. Charlie can't even remember her voice. Of course, we've got photos of his mother, but he never heard her talk." Bill's voice cracked, "That really upset Charlie when he got older, he was always asking me what her voice sounded like. She would have been a wonderful mother, and of course Charlie missed out on having any brothers and sisters. His only real family are me and his grandmother."

"That must have been so tough for you and Norah."

"Yes, it was, I was very angry and rejected Charlie for the first couple of months. Could hardly bring myself to look at him. I threw myself into my work and relied on Norah a lot. Too much, looking back. I just wish I could have given her the support she gave me. Then when Charlie was at that stage when they are tottering around like a little drunkard on two legs, he started choking on a of Lego one day. After a few sharp smacks on the back, he spat it out, but I thought I was going to lose him as he was turning blue and that's when we bonded. That horrid little incident made me realise that I was focusing all my pent-up anger on my son and that underneath it all, I really loved him."

Bill's eyes filled with tears at the memory.

"Did you ever want to get married again?" Milly enquired, softly.

"I had a couple of relationships and there was someone once. But Charlie was very protective of me which made it hard for her. Then there was Norah to consider. I felt I just couldn't present her with a replacement for her daughter. Besides, I'm not sure Charlie and his grandmother would have given anyone else their approval. It must be hard being a step-parent, don't you think?"

"Oh yes, I've got friends whose lives have been made a misery because they've been cast as the wicked step-parent."

They chatted on about their various friends' experiences of being step-parents until Bill's eye-lids started to droop and he was snoozing.

What a handsome man you are, Milly thought studying his features. She tried to picture what his wife looked like. Then quietly taking his tea cup, she left the room.

Charlie and Ciara were looking very cosy together the next morning at breakfast. Although they sat at separate tables, it didn't stop them chatting animatedly about the world of acting.

"So, do you miss 'Wellington Square'?" Ciara asked.

"Yes, it was great, and the cast were like family, but I'd been on the programme since I was eleven and didn't want to get typecast."

"That was brave, gosh, I'd love the security of being in a soap instead of going for auditions all the time." she sighed.

"Yeah, I know what you mean," Charlie answered, buttering another piece of toast. "We'll be in the 'Ship', around ten-thirty. Just in time for last orders, if you want to join us. Come and meet the cast."

"I might just do that," Ciara smiled, as her mobile pinged. "Right that's my taxi, better go."
Putting on her long gloves, she swept out of the room for another day thrilling the race-goers as Audrey Hepburn, at 'Glorious Goodwood'.

Bill was making a good, steady recovery. Charlie was very attentive, making sure his father had everything he needed, and every day before he left for his show, he ate with his father.
Around nine o'clock that night, as Charlie requested, Milly went to check on Bill. There was no reply when she knocked softly on the door.
What should I do? I don't want to intrude… Oh gosh, I'd better check, I told Charlie I would.
Opening the door softly, she peeped into the room. He was sound asleep. He'd eaten the food Charlie had left him, so Milly quietly took the tray away from his bedside table.
Well, you are a fine-looking man, no one would ever think you had just had a heart attack. Get better soon Bill, she whispered, resisting the urge to kiss his handsome cheek.
I bet you and Janey were a handsome couple. I wonder what she looked like.
Milly sighed as she exited his room.

Milly's wonderings about Janey were rudely interrupted by a persistent ring on the door bell.
Oh no not more guests.
This really was the worst part of running a ''B&B'', one was permanently on call. Just at that precise moment Milly had to stop herself slapping the 'No Vacancies' sign up on the door. But as tempting as this was, she reminded herself that she had bills to pay and they weren't cheap in a place like 'Willow Cottage'.

To her amazement, two burly men were standing at the door carrying a stretcher with a man lying on it.

"Evenin' Holly, darlin'," an elderly man with a broad Irish accent said, from under his blankets, "I've done me back in, so my two minders 'ere will take me upstairs to my room. What? Er, you're not Holly?"

"No, she moved to America, I'm Milly Henderson, the new owner."

"Righto, well I'm the bookie. Seamus O'Leary, is the name," he said extending his hand from under his blankets. "I come regular every year from Woodford Green in London, for 'Glorious Goodwood'.

Holly hadn't put anything in the Bookings book but Mr O'Leary clearly knew her and was familiar with 'Willow Cottage'. As she had some spare rooms she didn't have the heart to turn them away. So, inviting them in, the two burly minders started to negotiate the stairs up to the rooms. Milly heart was in her mouth as she watched them. Mr O'Leary was totally unfazed as they tilted the stretcher at various perilous looking angles but thankfully, they made it up the stairs and deposited Mr O'Leary in one piece in the Hibiscus room on the second floor.

" 'Ere you are lads, go and get yourselves a beer," he said giving them a crisp twenty-pound note.

"Thanks Guv, are we next door then missus?"

"Yes, the twin is free if you are alright in there?"

"Yup that's fine missus, got to keep an eye on our 'guvnor' here."

"There're good boys," Mr O'Leary smiled. "Take care of me good and proper. We'll be here for three nights. Breakfast at seven if that's okay darlin, we like to set off early and get set up."

Suppressing a smile, Milly said that was fine.

Thank God I stocked up on eggs and bacon. No doubt, they'll eat for England.

Chapter Eleven

They did eat for England. Milly had to make two extra racks of toast for Mr O'Leary's minders and her tea cups clearly weren't big enough. One gulp and their cup was empty. These lads clearly weren't familiar with the niceties of tea cups and saucers. She'd have to get some man-sized mugs.

Never mind, Milly liked them. They were just tucking into their bacon and eggs with gusto when a surprise visitor came into the dining room.

"Milly, you've got a pig in the house." Mr O'Leary called out to her in the kitchen. "Are you giving us a taster of our next breakfast?" he joked as she rushed in to the dining room.

"Oh, my goodness Dad, what are you doing in here? He must have got out of his bed," Milly started to explain, "He's my pet pig..."

"Pet pig?" One of the minders smirked.

"It's a long story," Milly said, scooping Dad up.

"What a delightful little fella, you're a real little beauty ain't ya darlin?" Mr O'Leary stroked Dad's snout.

"Ain't he gorgeous boys?"
They didn't look impressed.

"He's going to be a big'un...

"You think so?" Milly asked, starting to worry.

"Oh yes, you'll get a good coupla chops out of 'im! Don't you believe all they say about them Micro pigs not growing."

"Oh Dad, isn't a micro pig, he's a pot-bellied Vietnamese. My daughter was told he'll stay quite small."

"Nah, he's definitely going to be a big'un..."
There was no doubt that Dad had grown a lot bigger in the short time Milly had him.

He must have got out of his box and jumped down the high step from the ironing room. A giant pig running around. That's all I need. Trust Sophie ...

"Come on Rufus. Come in here with 'Dad'. We can't have him getting out into the dining room again."
Then, carefully rubbing some antiseptic hand gel into her hands after handling 'Dad', Milly made her way back to the kitchen. Mr O'Leary and his minders had left for the day and Charlie should be coming down any minute for his breakfast.

***

"Mrs H, something very strange happened last night." Charlie said as Milly gave him his poached eggs.
"Oh yes?"
"I was reading in bed when I saw the door handle turn on my door. There was no one there when I opened it. I thought I was imagining things and went back to bed but then it happened again."
"Maybe you nodded-off and didn't realise you were dreaming?"
Charlie pondered for a moment.
"Maybe …"
His misgivings were short lived because as soon as Ciara came into the dining room he seemed to forget all about it.

Milly thought no more about it either until Charlie said the same thing at breakfast the next morning.
"The door thing happened again last night, Mrs H."
"Sounds like a ghost to me," Ciara said, looking distinctly nervous.
"Now don't start frightening all my guests away," Milly reprimanded Charlie, "Don't worry dear," she directed to Ciara, "I've never heard or seen anything."
But Charlie, quietly adamant, stuck to his story.

***

Milly and Bill had slipped into the habit of having a small gin and tonic in his room every evening shortly after Charlie left for his show.

"Sounds like you should turn this place into a nursing home," Bill laughed when Milly related the antics about the two minders struggling to get Mr O'Leary upstairs on his stretcher.

"Funnily enough, I did think about that when I first came here. But then I started to enjoy doing 'B&B', besides there are so many health and safety rules, with 'Stannah' stair lifts etcctera, I thought the house would lose its charm… Did Charlie tell you about the incident with his door?" Milly asked, as she handed him his drink.

"Yes," Bill grinned. "Sounds like he's trying to get this young lady of yours to keep him company in the dead of night…"

"Well, I've never heard or seen anything," Milly said, "And I'm sure Rufus would sense something."

"Well, there you go then, he's trying to get into this young lady's knickers."

"Bill!"

"Boys will be boys," he winked.

"They do make rather a handsome couple," Milly smiled, "And they are both actors…"

"Yes, well sometimes that's good and sometimes it's bad." Bill elaborated. "If one gets a good part and the other doesn't, or there's too much romping on stage or screen with a glamorous co-star, that can be the death knell for a relationship."

"Yes, I can understand that," Milly agreed. "Right, duty calls, I'm off to feed 'Dad'," she announced, taking their empty glasses.

"Night Bill."

"Night Milly."

Around three in the morning, Charlie felt something tug the bottom of his duvet. He hadn't been sleeping well as he'd been keeping a watch on the door handle.
He tugged back, twice. Whoever or whatever it was, tugged back violently then kicked something across the room.

"Shit!" He shouted, leaping out of bed and racing across the room to put the light on. No one was there but his trainers had been kicked against the wardrobe. Pulling on his dressing gown, he raced up to his father's room and crept into the double bed next to him. Bill didn't even stir.

"Oh, it's you," Bill remarked the next morning.

"Yes, sorry Dad. Milly's going to have to move me out of that room. There's a poltergeist or something in there."

"You sure you didn't have one too many Son?"

"It kicked my trainers across the room and tugged my duvet. I tugged back as a test and it tugged right back."

"Maybe it was that pretty girl I'm hearing about."

"No, Dad, it wasn't Ciara, it was bloody terrifying. There's something in that room. Anyway, sorry I'm not Milly."

"Now one thing I am son, is a gentleman," Bill smiled.

Charlie was sitting next to Ciara when Milly brought their breakfast in. He got up a lot earlier, Milly noticed, now that the lovely Ciara was there. They were both having a good old belly laugh when Milly gave Ciara her fruit juice and cereal.

"Sorry Mrs Henderson. Go on, tell her," Ciara urged in between laughing.

"Well, no doubt you will hear soon enough Mrs H," Charlie said looking somewhat sheepish, "But last night I had to bunk in with my Dad. I think there's a poltergeist or something in my room."

"Oh, my goodness, Charlie, what happened?" Milly felt goose bumps down her spine as Charlie relayed the story.

"Do you think something happened in that room?" Ciara asked.

"I don't know. Before I turned it back into a bedroom, the previous owner used it as a sewing room. But before that it was once a school."

"A school? It must have been very small." Ciara remarked, looking surprised.

"Yes, I suppose so. It was a 'Penny School' in Victorian times. Poor children's parents paid a penny a week to have their children taught to read and write. The picture of the teacher and the children is still in there."

"Yes, I've seen it," Charlie added, turning white.

"Miss Gibbons, that's what she was called. The previous owner told me. I think she's buried in the churchyard," Milly said taking Charlie and Ciara's plates out to the kitchen.

"Let's have a séance tonight," Ciara whispered surreptitiously to Charlie. "Ask whoever it is what they want?"

Although a little unnerved at the thought of 'messing with the spirit world,' Charlie agreed. If that was what it took to get the lovely Ciara in his room...

"So, shall we do it then? All we need is a glass, a little table and a piece of paper with the alphabet written in a circle. I've got time after work, shall I set everything up?"

"Okay, I won't be back 'til after eleven though."

"Even better. Midnight, that's the perfect time! I'll meet you in the pub after the show. We might need a drink for Dutch courage," she joked. Then Ciara's phone pinged and she swished off to get her taxi.

"Look Charlie, I will move you into a different room," Milly said as she brought in his eggs and bacon. I can't have you being scared out of your wits like that."

"No rush Mrs H, maybe Rufus could come up with me."

"Er, well," Milly didn't like to admit that Rufus slept with her every night.

"Look, I might have imagined the whole thing, after all, I have been worried about Dad and…"

"No Charlie, I will move you into another room. I'll also get the vicar round, see what he can do."

Chapter Twelve

Milly had just loaded up the washing machine after clearing away Charlie and Ciara's breakfast dishes when the door-bell rang.

Oh no, not another punter, so early in the day. Why didn't people turn up later? Like they did in hotels. Maybe I should tell people not to check in before six at night…

"Hi, I'm Audrey, from 'The Old Sweet Shop 'B&B',' just over the road from you. Just thought I'd pop in and say hello. Are you the new owner?"

"Yes, I am, how do you do? I'm Milly. How nice to meet another Bed & Breakfast Queen!"

"Oh yes, very funny, I suppose that is what we are. 'B&B' Queens, I like that," she laughed heartily. She was a rather rotund little lady, who looked around fifty, with bleached-blonde hair and very black roots and she was very obviously angling to be asked in for a coffee.
So Milly did the polite thing and obliged.

"Come in, would you like a coffee?"

"Oh, yes please," she practically jumped in the door and followed Milly straight into the kitchen. "So, have you had many bookings over the Goodwood week?"

"Yes, it's been very busy," Milly answered as she made some fresh coffee. "I had a lot of calls from people wanting to book in. I've inherited quite a few regulars and also have a young actor staying for the run of his show at the Festival Theatre."
Audrey's face visibly dropped.

"Oh, so you turned people away?"

"Well yes, I had to. Oh goodness, Audrey, if I'd known you did 'B&B' I could have passed them on to you? I'll know next time…"

"Don't worry, I should have come over before now and introduced myself. But yes, Holly always sent people over to me if she was fully booked."

"Right, I will do the same. How about you? Have you been busy?"

"Oh yes, rushed off my feet." Audrey fibbed.

"That's a lovely house you have," Milly remarked. Was it really a sweet shop?"

"Yes, my grandparents sold sweets there for fifty odd years. We're real experts on old fashioned sweets in our family. Rhubarb crumbles, Flying Saucers, Midget gems, Parma Violets, you name, it, they sold it… So how much how much do you charge for a double? Do you charge less for a twin? How many choices do you give for breakfast?" The questions were fast and furious. Milly could hardly keep up with them. No sooner had she answered one, she was bombarded with another.

She's going to ask to see my rooms next.
And sure enough, she did.

Audrey wasn't showing any signs of going and Milly was starting to get distinctly annoyed.

"You must have heard that your predecessor married that famous racing driver? He was one of her guests."

"Yes, so I've heard. Audrey, I'm so sorry, but I've got a mountain of ironing and am expecting more guests tonight. Can we catch up another time? It's been really lovely to meet you..."
Milly stood up purposefully, hoping she'd take the hint.

"Oh, oh yes, of course, thank you for the coffee." Audrey mumbled, looking rather miffed.
As they made their way to the door, Audrey's eye caught sight of Milly's 'Visitors book' out on the little table by the front door.

"I see you've kept Holly's 'Visitors Book.' Have you had some nice comments?"

"I've been so busy, I haven't had a chance to look. Here's hoping they are as good as Holly's."

"Yes, well between ourselves, I heard on the grapevine that Holly's breakfasts weren't up to much. Apparently, she was a bit mean with the eggs and bacon." Before Milly could make any kind of answer, the landline rang.
Great, saved by the bell.

"So sorry, Audrey, must get the phone. Thank you for coming over."

It was Sophie.

"Dearie me, Sophie, I've just met another 'B&B' owner from across the road. She clearly wanted to see what goes on here. You should have heard the questions she asked me…"

"So, it's the battle of the 'B&B' Queens Mum?" Sophie laughed.

"Well, maybe on her part. Anyway, darling, how are you?"

There was a muffled silence on the phone.

"Soph??"

"Oh Mum," Sophie started to sob. "Lloyd says he isn't ready to be a father. What am I going to do?"

This had been happening with monotonous regularity since the start of Sophie's pregnancy and Milly knew it would probably all be sweetness and light next week. But that was small comfort. Lloyd was a little toe-rag and Milly was convinced their relationship wouldn't survive the demands of a new baby.

"Move down here darling, there's plenty of room."

"Thank you, Mum, that's so sweet. But I want to stay in London."

"Why dear? You could get a job down here, we could find a nursery for the baby, I'm here, you'd have support."

"I know Mum and thank you, but I love my flat."

"I know dear, but it's rented accommodation. Look, I'll make part of the house over to you."

"You need the rooms Mum."

"No, I don't. Not all of them. I could still do my 'B&B'. We'd manage…"

"Sorry Mum, got to go. Lloyd's ringing."

***

"I just want to scoop her up and bring her down here," Milly confided to Bill as they were having their early evening 'G&T'.

"I can imagine. I'd feel the same," Bill remarked, putting his hand affectionately over Milly's.

"You would?"

"Yes, I think I would."

The silence that ensued was oddly comforting. Neither needed to speak.

"Oh, sorry," Bill suddenly grimaced, pulling his hand away.

"Are you okay?" Milly panicked.

"Excuse me one moment."

To her horror, Bill stuck his finger in his mouth and pulled out plate with two false teeth on it which he jiggled about for a bit, then put back in his mouth.

"That's better, damned uncomfortable. Have to get back to the dentist, bloody thing doesn't fit. Now, where were we?"

Suppressing a giggle, Milly felt oddly comforted. If she and Bill ever kissed, confessing she had a plate with three falsies on it wouldn't be so bad because he clearly wasn't worried about his.

"Will she come down for a bit when she has the baby?"

"I don't know. I hope so. I want to be there for them."

"Things will work out, you'll see," he said patting her hand and looking deeply into her eyes. "I can go downstairs and out for a short ten-minute walk tomorrow."

"That's great Bill."

"Yes, Charlie and I are going to Tesco. Can't stand the place, I'm a Waitrose man."

"Yes, know what you mean." Milly laughed.

"He's banned me from carrying any bags."

"Good."

"I met a fellow 'B&B' owner today," Milly said pouring them another 'G&T'.

"That must have been interesting."

"Yes and no. She's from over the road. I think she was being nosey."

"From over the road?" Bill raised his eyebrows. "The Old sweet shop?"

"Yes."

"Charlie and I stayed there the first week of his rehearsals. Terrible place. Greasy bacon, tinned tomatoes, cold tea and half cooked toast…"

"Oh no, she probably thinks I'm pinching her guests…"

Bill's eyes were starting to droop and so Milly collected up his plate and their glasses and quietly exited the room.

She was busy feeding 'Dad' in the ironing room when she heard Charlie's key clattering in the door. There was a lot of laughter and giggling as he and Ciara came in to the hall. It had taken them two or three attempts to open the door. Tripping up the stairs together they'd obviously had a good night.

"Come in," Charlie whispered, switching on the light into his old room where he'd had the creepy experience.

"Cup of tea?" he asked going over to the kettle in the corner of the room. "Sugar?"

"No, I'm sweet enough," Ciara teased as she pulled out a pile of cut up letters from her handbag. All neatly secured together with a large paper clip. Charlie put a glass in the middle of the table while she arranged the letters in a circular alphabet with the words 'Yes' and 'No' on each side of the circle.

"You sure you're up for this?" he asked, as he handed Ciara her tea.

"You're not chickening out, are you?" she asked, teasingly.

"Course not," he said, taking a gulp of tea.

Ciara brought an extra chair in from her room. Charlie dimmed the lights to create a more intimate, ghost-friendly atmosphere, then they both sat down and delicately put a finger lightly on the upturned glass.

"You have to swirl the glass thirteen times around the board," Ciara announced authoritively.

Charlie followed her lead, then took a deep breath and asked in his most theatrical voice:

"Miss Gibbons, are you there? Was is it you who threw my expensive Nike trainers across the room?"
Silence.
Ciara had her eyes closed, her head tilted up towards the ceiling. Charlie could see the rise and fall of her chest and that lovely cleavage...

"Miss Gibbons are you there?" he repeated.
The glass moved slowly towards "Yes."

"Now we're getting somewhere," Ciara said excitedly, her voice at least one octave higher than usual.
Charlie wasn't so ecstatic.
Then the glass suddenly went berserk, jerking across the table. It was so fast they couldn't read the letters.

"Oh my god," Ciara screamed.

"Oh shit!" Charlie exclaimed grabbing her hand and pulling her up from the table. "Let's get out of here."
Bolting into Ciara's room, they slammed the door.

"Was it you? You moved the glass, didn't you?"

"God no, you saw what happened."
Charlie put a protective arm around her. Scared out of his wits he knew he had to be the big strong, macho male.

"The glass, it went crazy didn't it?" Ciara said, her big blue eyes as wide as saucers.

"Yeah, it was mad."

"Charlie I'm scared."
Charlie pulled her closer.

"You'll be okay, there's nothing in here. Thank God Mrs H moved me out of that room."

"You're staying with me tonight," Ciara snuggled closer.

"I am?"

"Yes. A damsel in distress and all that…"

"*Thank you, Miss Gibbons,*" Charlie whispered as he got to know Ciara a lot better.

Not wanting to advertise the fact that he'd spent the night in Ciara's room, Charlie carefully peeked round her door before creeping back into his room the next morning.

"See you at breakfast," Ciara teased, "Oh, don't forget these," she laughed throwing him his underpants.

Mm, they're getting very friendly, Milly mused as she brought in their breakfast. They were now sharing a table every morning.

"Mrs H, I've got a bit of a confession to make." Charlie said after Ciara had left in her taxi.

"Oh, yes? It can't be that bad. Can it?" Milly asked good-naturedly as she collected his plates.

"Er, well, Ciara and I had a séance last night – you know, when you put a glass on the table…"
Milly's face dropped.

"Oh, what happened?" She asked in a dead pan voice.

"Well, the glass started going berserk and…"

"You shouldn't mess around with these things you know."

"Sorry Mrs H. Do you think it was that school-teacher, Miss Gibbons?

"Maybe," Milly answered pensively. "I've been told that an old woman in a long black dress and bonnet has been seen walking up the outside staircase to that room."

Chapter Thirteen

Milly spent the whole morning surfing the internet for a psychic to 'cleanse' the 'Ghost Room,' as they referred to it now. Luckily, she struck gold and a Miss Longley, was coming after lunch.

Right on time, the doorbell rang. It was a rather preppy, serious-looking girl in her early twenties, who turned out to be Debbie Longley.

"Come in, I'm, so pleased you could make it so quickly."

The girl was looking up at one of the bedroom windows and appeared to be in a world of her own.

"I've just seen a face at an upstairs window. A woman with a very white face and long dark hair?"

Milly's heart sank. *Oh goodness, I hope she isn't a fraud. I bet she's read that book.*

When Milly moved in, Holly had left her a copy of a book she'd found in a Chichester bookshop entitled 'Haunted Chichester and Beyond'.

'Willow Cottage' was mentioned twenty odd years ago when a Mrs Sheila Darvil ran it as a 'B&B'. One of her guests reported that as they were walking up the garden path to the house late one night, they saw that the curtains in their room had been opened. A light was on and a strange lady with long dark hair was standing near the window in their room. Sheila told them that she had no other guests that night and when she went outside and looked up at the window, no-one was there.

Just like Sheila, Milly stepped outside and looked up at the window in question. She couldn't see anyone.

"That's strange, I haven't got anybody booked into that room. Please, come in."

The girl didn't immediately respond, hung back and appeared to be mesmerized by the window. Inviting her to come in again, she led her into the dining room where they sat down and had a quick cup of tea while Milly told her about the history of Charlie's old room.

"The previous owner told me she heard noises in that room. Apparently, an old lady has been seen going up the outside staircase which leads into the room. She thought it could be Miss Gibbons, the old school ma'am."

"It's good that you called me, Mrs. Henderson. People should never fool around with Ouija boards."

"I know," Milly agreed. "It was one of my guests. I'm not happy."

"Can you show me the room?"

"Yes of course, follow me."

As they went into Charlie's old room, they saw the cut-up letters of the alphabet strewn across the table. Some had fallen on the floor and the glass was lying on its side.

"There are many reasons why a Spirit might be trapped." Debbie explained. "They could be emotionally attached to the property or they might have had a traumatic death and never passed over because they are stuck and don't realise what's happened."

Placing her hands on the table, she took three deep breaths.

"I can feel a presence… Sometimes spirits need help crossing over to the other side... They don't see the light that is always there. With any Spirit, whether it's a Resident Spirit, a Free Roaming Spirit, or a Loved one who comes to say 'Hi,' the light is always there behind them. But the trapped ones just can't see it, even though they know it's there. Everything in death fights to get to the light eventually. When they are ready to see it, they will. That's when it's our duty to help cross them over."

Opening her Cath Kidson bag, Debbie took out a candle, a box of matches and a bell. She then turned off her mobile phone and asked Milly to switch the plugs off in the room. After closing the curtains, she lit the candle. Sitting very quietly she closed her eyes.

"Milly, I want you to close your eyes and imagine the door to this room is opening. As it opens in your mind's eye, you will hear me ask for 'Protection of the White Light.' I will ask for strength and guidance in sending over the lost souls in your home…"

As Debbie lit the candle, Milly closed her eyes and imagined the door to Charlie's room opening and Miss Gibbons scurrying out.

Debbie rang the bell, slightly startling Milly from her visualization.

"Miss Gibbons come to the light."
Debbie kept ringing the bell, and after what felt like an eternity, Milly opened her eyes and saw that the flame on the candle had started to jump and flicker.

"Miss Gibbons, come to the light. There is love in this room, come to the light. Follow the light Miss Gibbons, your children are waiting for you… they are all there on the other side. It is time that you followed them. You have been trapped in this room, but now you need to cross to the other side. You have been too long on this plain. Follow the light… whatever it is you fear on the other side isn't true. Look, look at the light… see… there are your children waiting for you, go to them now… be free and be at peace. God loves you and he wants you home. Don't fear home, it is beautiful and one day I will see you there but now isn't my time, it is yours'. Go, go to the light now, be free."

The candle had flickered violently but now, as it calmed, Debbie gently blew it out and wafted the smoke around the room with her hand, careful not to dispel the psychic energy in the room.

"Milly, please close your eyes again. I am going to count backwards from ten. During this time, I want you to imagine the door closing When I get to one, the door will be closed. 10-9-8-7-6-5-4-3-2-1… I ask Spirit to bless me with the White Light and bless this house and all the people in this house with the white light and all the people who enter this house with the white light. I call on my ancestors to make sure nothing enters me, this house or all the people I love and care for and to guide the person that I just sent home."

A couple of minutes passed. Debbie was perspiring and breathing heavily.

"She's gone, she was looking for one of her school children and hadn't realise that they had all passed to the other side. She said she felt guilty that she was always so horrid to him."

A peaceful sense of calm filled the room.

"Thank you so much Debbie."

"It's okay," she said as she was putting away her things. "I'm on holiday from uni, so its lucky you caught me. She has gone now."

As they were exiting the room, they bumped into Charlie and Bill coming up the stairs from their trip to Tesco.

"Debbie here has just helped release Miss Gibbons from your room Charlie."

Bill looked completely non-plussed.

"Was it you who used the Ouija board?"

Charlie quaked under Debbie's perceptive stare.

"Not a good idea," she said very firmly, "Especially if under the influence of alcohol, you never know what trouble you can attract. You should never mess with the spirit world."

"Oh no, I won't. Thank you."

"You were lucky this time."

Charlie was actually blushing and shifting uncomfortably from foot to foot. Giving him a reproving look, Milly saw Debbie to the door, thanking her profusely, she gave her the agreed donation to the local spiritualist church plus a little extra.

"Phew, I think I need a gin and tonic."

"It's only three o'clock Mrs H."

"Well its seven o'clock somewhere in the world. How was your walk Bill?"

"Good, feel a bit tired now tho."

"You were only meant to go out for a ten-minute walk."

"We had a coffee in Tesco," Charlie added. "I'm really sorry about the Ouija board thing Mrs H. Won't happen again."

He really was far too charming to get cross with.
Again.

***

The lovely Ciara had gone and Charlie was pining.
She'd confessed that she had a boyfriend when he saw her
off on the train earlier that afternoon. Apparently, Miss
Gibbons and the heebie-jeebies had got to her.
Ah well, you win some and you lose some, Charlie
reflected as the make-up girls worked their magic before
the show. But a little piece of his heart was broken.
It would have been good to get together with Ciara.
A fellow actor who knew what it was like to go for all
those soul-destroying auditions, never knowing when the
next paycheck was coming or if you were going to ever
tread the boards again.
Ah, Ciara...

Chapter Fourteen

Two weeks had gone by and Bill was a lot better. He'd increased his walking by ten minutes every other day. In a week's time he would be back at work as musical director and lead cellist for a prestigious London orchestra.

"So, how do you feel about going back to work?" Milly asked that evening as she took up a tray of ice and lemon for their drinks.

"It will be good, I think I'll take it easy for the first couple of days... get back into the swing of things so to speak, but I will miss you Milly," he said holding her with his eyes and patting the edge of his bed for her to sit down." All your crazy stories about ghosts, pet pigs and unhinged guests…
Milly's heart missed a beat.

"I will miss you too Bill. I'll have to get Charlie into drinking 'G&T's'."

"Do you think you could get away one day and come to one of my concerts? You've been so kind, I don't know what Charlie and I would have done without you."

"That would be lovely, I'm sure Sophie would come down and hold the fort."

"Great, I'm conducting a new piece by the celebrated composer, Pete Harris, at St. Martins-in-the-Fields, two weeks from now. Starts at Seven-thirty. I'll take you to dinner at 'Gianni's' afterwards. It's one of my favourite places to eat. Oh goodness, think that walk's taken it out of me…"

His eyes were closing. Milly waited a few minutes and when she thought he was asleep she kissed him gently on the cheek. Unbeknown to her, Bill smiled as she exited the room.

Milly was so happy she picked 'Dad' out of his box and did a little jig around the room with him.

"Dad'! I've got a date."

***

It had all been arranged. Sophie was coming down to 'Willow Cottage' for the night and Bill was leaving a ticket in the box office for Milly to pick up just before the performance. As he was musical director, he was conducting the orchestra that night in their performance of *'The Fallen Angel'*. They'd meet after the show and go out to dinner. Then Milly would stay the night with her friend, Sasha in Chiswick.

"Now, are you sure you will manage dear? Brett, the man in the 'Foxglove' room has breakfast at nine. Just toast and cereal. He's been here a week now. Thinking of moving to Chichester apparently. Charlie has breakfast at eight; a full 'English' usually. Cook the sausages first, then the bacon, he likes a hash brown and…

"A cooked tomato … Yes, Mum, it will be fine - I can manage. I will walk Rufus after breakfast and then tidy Charlie's and the other guy's rooms. If any punters check in off the street, I will take their car registration and make them pay upfront."

"Oh no, dear. I don't want you taking anybody in off the road, far too risky, you never know who you are letting into your house."

"You do it."

"Yes, well you are a young girl, here on your own. Please, darling, just for me, put the 'No Vacancies' sign up and just look after Charlie and Mr Ponytail."

"Mr Ponytail?"

"The guy in the Foxglove. He's quite a character, sports a little ponytail and has lots of colourful tattoos."

"Sounds interesting."

"Yes, you'll like him. Very chatty. Seems to know a lot about antiques. Take 'Dad' out in the garden for a wee ten minutes after a feed. You've got his rota, haven't you?"

"Yes, everything will be fine Mum. You look lovely by the way, really pretty."

"Oh Soph, this isn't a date!" Milly laughed nervously.

"What is it then?"

"Just a friendly meeting."

"Mum, it's okay, I'm happy for you. He sounds nice." Stupidly, Milly felt as if their roles had been reversed. Sophie was the sensible mother figure and she was the rebellious young daughter straining at the leash...

Parking her car at the station, she caught the train to Victoria then jumped on a tube to Turnham Green.

***

"Milly, you look great, you've lost weight," Sasha exclaimed kissing her friend on the cheek."

"Yes, think it's climbing all those stairs and making beds."

"You've had Botox, you look ten years younger."

"Botox? God no, I've no time, even if I wanted to, wouldn't mind having some though," Milly laughed, tweaking her cheeks.

"You don't need it." Sasha said giving her a cup of tea. "So, have you kissed yet?"

"God no! The thought terrifies me. I mean, how do you tell someone you have a plate? Having said that though, he's got one."

"How do you know?"

"He took it out in front of me."

"Well, he clearly feels very comfortable with you."

"Yes, but snogging and false teeth, well, somehow they don't seem to go…"

"No, they don't do they?" Sasha chuckled. "Get some implants, you must be raking the money in with all that hard work."

"Don't know about that, the house costs a fortune to run."

"Yes, I can imagine. Still think you should treat yourself though. It's not as if you need a whole set…"

"Sasha, darling, if we do ever get that close he can just accept me as I am. Wrinkles, stretch marks and all..."

A couple of hours later, Milly was on the tube to Charing Cross. As she walked into the church and picked up her ticket, the butterflies fluttered in her stomach. The church was bathed in candle light with that lovely 'church' smell, of polish and incense permeating the expectant atmosphere. The young orchestra, all dressed smartly in their obligatory black suits, bow ties and evening dresses were quietly tuning up their instruments as people took their seats. Milly realized that this was the first time she had gone out to a concert on her own. It felt odd not having Jack at her side. She felt acutely aware of couples chatting and checking the programme together then reminding each other to switch off their mobile phones.

Bill made his entrance.

Milly thought her heart would stop as she watched him bow to the clapping audience. Dressed in an impeccable black evening suit and bow tie, his dark, greying, shaggy hair, a little rebellious contrast to his formal attire.

"Ladies and gentleman, a very warm welcome to everybody here in this beautiful church of St Martin's-in-the-fields." The rich timbre of his voice echoed warmly throughout the church. "And a huge thank you to those of you who have made the journey from outside London," he added, catching Milly's eye.

The audience's chatter had died down to a murmur then fell silent as he raised his baton. All the orchestras' young eyes were on Bill.

As he brought his baton down, the first notes, played by a viola, broke sweetly through the silence.

Bill had a wonderfully charismatic aura on stage.

It must have been such a thrill for him and his wife to work together.

Milly could just picture her in a beautiful black, silk concert dress, their eyes feasting on one another as they surrendered themselves to the music...

It was a wonderful, intimate performance and Milly was even brave enough to leave her seat and mingle with the crowd for a glass of wine in the interval.

As she took her seat for the second half of the concert, Milly couldn't help wondering if the other couple of single-looking women in the audience were there for the music as much as for the handsome conductor. But those thoughts were soon chased away by Bill's mesmerizing performance.

The music gathered pace and rose through a crescendo to the final crashing chord, and before she knew it, the concert was over. The church resounded with applause from the delighted audience as Bill bowed and then acknowledged his orchestra before exiting the stage.

Milly's heart was in her mouth as she waited for him in the foyer. His formal attire swapped for his usual jeans and jumper, Bill kissed Milly on the cheek and put his arm protectively around her while acknowledging various congratulatory messages from his audience. Guiding her out of the church into the buzzing atmosphere of Trafalgar Square, Bill flagged down a black cab.

"Oh Bill, that was wonderful."

"Glad you enjoyed it," He said looking into her eyes, his arm still around her in the back of the cab. "I hope you're hungry. I'm ravenous, it's all that waving around."

Moments later they stepped into a delightful French restaurant in Soho. The 'Maître D' clearly knew Bill well and directed them to a lovely little table in a cosy corner of the restaurant. After their obligatory gin and tonic, they ordered their food. Boeuf Bourguignon for Bill and Moules Marinière and Pommes Frites for Milly.

"So, how are you Bill?"

"I'm okay, I get tired but other than that, I'm fine. It's good to get back into a routine and Charlie's culinary efforts, bless him, were starting to affect my waistline. So, what's been going on at 'Willow Cottage'?" he teased, pouring Milly a glass of wine.

"Well, I'm pleased to say Miss Gibbons hasn't come back yet, and now that the lovely Ciara has gone, I don't think breakfast is as exciting for Charlie now."

"Yes, I think he had a soft spot for her. Sounds like she has a boyfriend tucked away."

"Oh no, poor Charlie."

"He'll get over it. Now, how about you? How are you getting to grips with the solo existence?"

"I'm okay. It felt funny going to a concert on my own. First time in forty odd years."

"You'll get used to it," he said taking her hand across the table. "It's difficult at first, suddenly not doing things as a couple, takes time."

"Did it take you long to adjust to doing things on your own?"

"Yes and no. I threw myself into my work, but yes, I remember feeling horribly guilty when I went out on my first date. It must have been a good five years after Janey died, I felt like some awful adulterer. Silly really, because even Norah thought it was time for me to start living my life again."

"What was she like…? Janey, I mean…" Milly asked tentatively.

"Beautiful. Impulsive. A little crazy on occasion. Too young to die."

There was a palpable silence in the air only broken when the waiter brought the menu for dessert.

"She was a flautist, and a very good one. That's how we met, we were part of the same orchestra. I was lead cellist at the time. Could never play for them again after she died. Everybody knew us as a couple and I couldn't bear to see her place taken by another musician."

"I can understand that. Is Charlie like her?"

"Yes, same dark hair and eyes. Similar bone structure. He was a cruel physical reminder of Janey. I think that's why I was so dismissive of him when he was really young."

"You've clearly made up for it. He adores you."

"I know. I'm very lucky. It could have been so different. But that was all a long time ago. I don't know about you, but I'm desperate for some dessert."

Talk turned to the shenanigans of 'Willow Cottage'. They were the last to leave the restaurant and Bill insisted on getting Milly a cab home. After a friendly peck on the cheek, they said goodbye, agreeing to meet again soon. Milly's heart sank as she watched him walk away into the night.

We got on so well. Should we have kissed? What happens now?

Sasha was still up when Milly let herself in.

"Well?"

Milly felt decidedly flat.

"I wasn't sure if you'd be back tonight."

"Well, here I am."

"Did you think he'd whisk you back to his place?"

"Well… yes."

Sasha placed two cups of tea on the table as she looked at her friend.

"You like him, don't you?"

"I do." Milly was reluctant to admit it.

How can I be attracted to another man so soon after losing Jack?

"Things will happen in their own time Milly. And well, maybe he's a gentleman?"

As she sat on the train on the way back to Chichester the next morning, she replayed the evening over and over again. The way he looked at her when he came out on to the stage, the way he took her hand across the table, then that measured peck on the cheek, what did it all mean?

Chapter Fifteen

Sophie was busy hoovering the dining room when Milly arrived back at the house.

"God Mum, no wonder you've lost weight. I'm exhausted going up and down the stairs and making beds."

"Making beds?"

"Yes, I booked some people into the family room last night."

"Sophie..."

"Don't worry, they are really nice and loved their breakfast. I got them to pay upfront," she said proudly, patting the lid on the ceramic chicken egg-holder where Milly kept her cash payments. "So, how did it go then?"

"Good darling, we had a really nice time."

"And?"

"And what?"

"When are you seeing him again?"

"Well that's just it. I don't know."

"You don't know?"

"We didn't actually arrange anything."

"He'll probably be down again to see Charlie though, won't he?"

"I don't know darling. I suppose so, he's seen his show a couple of times already."

As Sophie continued flicking her duster, Milly could tell her daughter thought it was odd they hadn't made another arrangement.

"Oh Mum, by the way, Mr Ponytail asked if his girl-friend could come down tonight. I said that was okay and moved him into the Gardenia room. He's paid up to last night, so don't forget to charge him again tomorrow. She's coming sometime this afternoon."

As Milly was making a note, reminding herself to charge them, the young family Sophie had booked in came down the stairs with their bags.

"Thank you for a lovely breakfast, we've had a very comfortable stay."

"My pleasure," Sophie beamed. "You've got competition Mum; my breakfasts are as good as yours – she doesn't trust me you know."

"Aw, she did really well. Even Ryan here, ate everything."

They were indeed a lovely little family. Despite the fact that little Ryan had wet the bed and peeled off a chunk of wallpaper.

Mr Ponytail's girlfriend, who arrived a little later, was as much as a character, in her own way, as he was. A good ten years or so older than Brett, she was a rather glam fifty-something lady, with lots of blonde hair styled into a nineteen-fifties style quiff.

"Hello," she said, beaming at them, while coming in with her bags "I'm Gabriella. Don't mind my fish tail, I'm swimming at a Mer-people convention in Brighton tomorrow and this is my mermaid tail."

"Oh wow! it's beautiful," Sophie exclaimed, stroking the emerald green sequins.

"My word, it's gorgeous, let me help you with your bags and show you to your room. You've done enough now Soph, go and sit down... My daughter's pregnant," Milly explained.

"Oh, how lovely, well, 'dolphin kicks' are great for the core. Just the way to get back into shape after having a baby. It's the way we are taught to swim, like a mermaid," she added, demonstrating the moves.

"Looks like fun."

"It is. Brett and I will be going to the pub tonight, if you want to join us. I can tell you all about it. I think he wants to buy your Mum a drink to thank her for looking after him."

"How nice, I'm sure Mum would love that. Maybe see you a little later then?"

"Sure, around seven okay?"

"Sounds good." Sophie replied.

"Pregnancy suits you darling, you've got that lovely bloom." Milly remarked proudly as they sat down for a coffee.

"So how is Lloyd? Is he more used to the idea of being a father now?"

Sophie cradled her cup of coffee.

"I dunno Mum. Hard to say."

"Well, I might not let you go back, my lovely, little pregnant pussy cat," she said, planting a kiss on Sophie's head as she made her way back into the kitchen for more coffee. "And you know I'm going to be a very demanding grandmother."

Sophie clearly didn't want to talk about how things were with her and Lloyd and so Milly suggested a trip around the baby shops.

It was lovely spending time together.

Would things have been different if I'd stayed in London? Milly mused as she picked up the tiniest pair of dungarees in Baby Gap. *Maybe Sophie would have moved back home. We would have managed and I would have been a real part of my grandchild's life. She won't leave London though - or that wimp of a boyfriend..."*

They were just coming in from the car with all the baby paraphernalia when they bumped into Mr Ponytail and Gabriella coming down the stairs.

"We're just off to the pub now for something to eat. Hope you are going to join us for a drink a bit later?" Gabriella asked.

"Sophie will be there," Milly said. "She's earned a drink after all her hard work."

"Mum, I'm not supposed to be drinking."

"Oh, sorry dear, I forgot. Didn't stop me..."

"Yes, well that was you."

After they'd had a little bite to eat, Milly busied herself laying tables for breakfast and seeing to 'Dad' while Sophie went to the pub. An hour or so later, Brett came back and knocked on the dining room door.

"Milly, why don't you join us? Let me buy you a drink to say thank you for all those delicious breakfasts." Milly didn't really want to go but since Sophie was pregnant, she found herself fretting about her and so agreed to go for one drink. Then she'd insist her 'little pregnant pussy cat' came home.

Gabriella and Sophie were ensconced in a cosy corner of the pub. Sophie was drinking a lemonade while Gabriella had what looked like a Martini cocktail. Brett went to the bar to get Milly a gin and tonic then teamed up with a few regulars at the pool table.

"Well ladies, I'll leave you in the land of the Mer-people," he said, refreshing their drinks and draining a beer after his game. "Think I'll go back to the house and do a little research on this lovely area."

"Watch the Martini's darling," he said, giving Gabriella a peck on the cheek "You've got your Tidal gathering tomorrow."

What a nice couple they are, Milly reflected as he deposited their drinks. *Mr. Ponytail is quite the gentleman…*

It was after eleven when they got back to the house. It had been a good evening and Sophie was already deciding on what colour fish-tail she'd get once she'd had the baby.

"If only she'd move down here Rufus, we'd love that, wouldn't we old boy?" Milly said as she switched off the light and snuggled under her single bed sheets.

Chapter Sixteen

Nine a.m. came and went and Brett and Gabriella hadn't made an appearance for breakfast.

"That's odd," Sophie remarked, "Gabriella's got her 'Tidal Gathering' at eleven. They're cutting it a bit fine. Do you think we should wake them up Mum?"

"Let's leave it until ten."

Ten came and went and still no sign. Their fruit juice and cereal were ready on a tray, the bacon, sausages and eggs waiting to be cooked. Sophie had been wandering around the house, chatting to Lloyd on her phone while Milly was hovering around the kitchen waiting to leap into 'Bed & Breakfast Queen' mode.

"Mum, did you move that picture Dorothea gave you?" Sophie asked as she wandered back into the kitchen.

"No. Why?"

"It's gone."

"What?"

Milly raced into the sitting room. The picture wasn't there. Mother and daughter looked at each other in perplexed shock. It was valuable, given to Milly by her great aunt, Dorothea, an accomplished concert pianist who lived with her lady-friend in a fantastic flat in the heart of London's West End and had many an adoring, unsuspecting, male admirer.

"You can have this dear," she'd said to Milly, just after she and Jack got engaged. *"Hold on to it, it's worth a pretty penny."*

Milly suddenly felt sick to the stomach.

"Mum, I hate to say it, but the sculpture on the piano has gone too."

"Oh my God, Sophie!"

"Sit down Mum, I'd better just see if Brett and Gabriella have come down for breakfast."

They weren't sitting expectantly in the dining room and there was no sign of them when Sophie went upstairs to knock on their door. Neither of them were in the bathroom or loo on that floor. Peeking inside their room, Sophie saw that they'd gone. Rushing down the stairs she noticed that the antique rocking-horse on the landing was missing. Her heart in her mouth, she ran outside to see if their car was there.

"Mum. They've gone! She said breathlessly as she walked purposefully into the sitting room where Milly was still sitting in shock.

"What?" Milly asked in disbelief.

"They've gone. So has the rocking horse. I bet it was them."

"I can't believe it."

"Neither can I, the shits. They must have had it all planned. That's why they wanted us to go to the pub. He must have snooped around when he came back to the house. Remember? Made Gabriella keep us entertained in the pub."

"Oh Sophie, this is dreadful."

"I know, oh Mum," Sophie said putting her arm around her mother. "We'd better call the police."

The police came and took a statement. Milly gave them the car registration number they had signed in with.

"False number plates," the officer said gravely after checking with the DVLA. He then picked up the waste-paper basket in the room they'd stayed in and pulled out a false pony tail and some scrunched up, stick-on tattoos. Both Milly and Sophie gasped in shock.

"This is always their little parting gesture. I'm afraid they are well known to the police on the south coast. They target 'B&B's and small hotels; befriending the owners, then when the coast is clear, they strike."

"Talk about sticking two fingers up at us." Sophie started to cry.

"But I would have heard their car driving down the drive, I'm a light sleeper." Milly interjected, hopelessly.

"He would have moved the car when you were in the pub. You need to be careful Mrs Henderson. Another

'B&B' owner in this area was duped by a man posing as a very convincing American. He broke down one morning over breakfast saying he had received a call in the middle of the night from his son in America, informing him that his wife and daughter had been killed in a car crash. After getting out the brandy, the 'B&B' owners paid for a taxi to take him directly to Gatwick airport and even gave him thirty pounds in cash so he wouldn't have the stress of finding a cashpoint machine. He put on a very convincing performance and the owners were so traumatised by his so-called loss, they didn't charge him a penny for his three-night stay. He probably didn't even go to Gatwick either, just took the money and booked himself into the next 'B&B' on his list, nasty piece of work. Anyway, I doubt you will hear from these two again, but I would advise you to change your locks."

"No need." Sophie said holding up the keys to the house and room, which they'd left on the bed.

"Well, at least they didn't go off with my keys," Milly remarked in a flat tone.

"Mum please be careful, I can't believe this has happened," Sophie said after the police had gone, Are you alright?"

"Yes, darling," Milly sighed. "I'm starting to realise that there's a lot more to running a 'B&B'."

"I don't want to leave you Mum," Sophie said as Milly drove her to the station with her bags.

"Don't be silly darling, I will be fine. I'm not on my own, Charlie is here."

"I know, but..."

"Sophie, I will be fine. I am more worried about you. Don't forget to call me when you get home."

"I won't Mum."

As Milly watched her take her seat on the train and wave at her through the window she forced herself not to cry. Sophie felt the same.

Chapter Seventeen

Bill did come down again.
He just showed up out of the blue one morning a few weeks later.

"Bill," what a lovely surprise, Milly beamed as she opened the door to him.

"I was just passing through and thought I'd stop to say hello. You busy?" he grinned, kissing her on the cheek.

"I've got Zac for a couple of days, and a family booked in tonight but other than that, no, come in."

"Well if you haven't any plans perhaps we can take him out somewhere? It's a nice day, a walk on the beach maybe?"

"That would be lovely… Zac, come here darling," she called up the stairs. "Would you like to go to the beach?" He'd been on the PlayStation all morning while Milly did the rooms. It would be a relief to have somebody to help get him out.
Stuck into his game, the child resolutely ignored her.
Bill caught on quickly.

"PlayStation?"

"How did you guess?"

"Charlie was the same," he smiled. "Shall I go up and say hello?"

"Of course, follow me."

"Hey, Mario Kart, can I play young man?"
Zac didn't hesitate in handing over a spare controller.
Bill played well and asked all the right questions about the game and was soon invited by Zac to play again.

"This is a really good game," Bill winked at Milly, "Excuse us for a moment."
Milly went downstairs to do some ironing and about twenty minutes later they both came down together.

"Bill said we can go to the beach," The little boy said excitedly. "He said its bad to be on the screen all day."
The little… how many times have Sophie and I told him that?

Half an hour later they were all walking along the golden sands of West Witterings beach. It was a beautiful day and there wasn't a cloud in the sky. Little Zac happily skipped between Milly and Bill, picking up shells and getting them to hold his hand and swing him along the beach. They'd bought a bucket and spade for him on the way, then erected a couple of the folding beach chairs Milly brought from the house, while Zac made a sand-castle. Rufus at Milly's feet, running back and forth into the waves.

"I'm shocked Milly," Bill remarked when she told him about her unfortunate experience with Brett and his mermaid. "You need some CCTV cameras outside the house. What a nasty experience for you and Sophie."

"Yes, it's a horrible feeling when you realise you're being befriended by calculating criminals under your roof. There's no doubt they had everything planned. His girl-friend really worked on getting Sophie to the pub with all her stories about 'morphing into mermaids.' The awful thing is, we really liked them…"

True to his word, Bill went straight into Chichester to enquire about installing CCTV cameras after dropping them back at the house. A couple of hours later he was back, balancing four or five boxes as he came through the front door.

"Oh my God, Bill!" Milly exclaimed. "You've got them already. I thought I'd have to get someone round."

"No need," Bill said pulling up his shirt sleeves. "I got them from the camera shop. The guys went through everything with me. Shouldn't take long. A cup of tea would be nice though." He winked.

How refreshing. A man fixing things for me.

Jack was useless at anything practical and always left any 'D.I.Y' to Milly. For the first time in her life she had an inkling about what it must be like having a man to take care of things for you. And it was a nice feeling. Bill was also a natural with kids. Jack had been good but Milly had noticed that on occasion his patience with his son was starting to wear a little thin. As she watched Bill showing Zac the equipment and poring over the instructions she realised she was falling in love.

This is too good to be true, Men like Bill must have his pick of women. All those talented, young musicians he was surrounded with. Why would he go for boring old Milly Henderson?

Charlie came into the house with Ciara, just as Bill was coming in from the garden with his tools and tea cup. To Charlie's delight, she'd turned up unexpectedly at 'Willow Cottage' that afternoon. They'd been for a walk across the fields putting 'their world to rights' and Ciara looked prettily pink in that youthful way, after her exertions.

"Dad, this is a surprise," Charlie said giving his father a hug. "This is Ciara, I don't think you two have been properly introduced."

"No, we haven't." Bill said extending his hand. "Hello Ciara, what's a gorgeous young girl like you see in my crazy actor son?"

"Well, I'm an actor too, so…" she tripped over her words and blushed. "I recently had a little job at Goodwood..."

"Yes, and she made a very lovely Audrey Hepburn," Milly cut in.

"'Breakfast at Tiffany's' – one of my favourite films," Bill remarked.

"Would you two like to join us for dinner?" Milly asked.

Ciara looked at Charlie.

"Thanks Milly, but we're meeting some of the cast in the pub. Probably eat at the Italian around the corner."

"Okay, well no more séances."

"Oh, no of course not," Ciara blushed. "I'm terribly sorry about that Mrs Henderson, it was my silly idea."

"Well, we don't want to invite Miss Gibbons back now, do we?"

"No, we don't," Charlie smiled, taking Ciara's hand as they went out the door.

"Looks like they are back together again," Milly remarked as she and Bill sat down with a glass of wine.

"Let's hope he doesn't get his heart broken again," Bill sighed, He's a bit of a softie, young Charlie."

"I do hope not," Milly sighed.

"Apparently she broke it off with the boyfriend. Feels she and Charlie have more in common."

"Well that's good, I'd hate to see him being mucked around," Milly commented. "Young love eh?"

"Indeed," Bill replied, holding her with his eyes.

Milly's casserole was bubbling away nicely in the kitchen and little Zac was playing with 'Dad' in the ironing room. There was a lovely aura of peace and calm.

"Thank you so much for today Bill," Milly said as she put a garlic and rosemary dipping oil and hot crusty bread on the table. "It was lovely to get out to the beach and it did Zac the world of good."

"Don't be silly, it was great for me too. I've missed being around little kids and it's always good to get rid of some of those London cobwebs."

"Ooh, garlic bread, can I give some to 'Dad'?" Zac asked as he brought in his little piggy bundle.

"Well, what do we have here? Bill asked.

"My piggy, his name is 'Dad'."

" 'Dad', what a great name. What a splendid little fellow."

"Here, you can hold him."

Bill carefully took the piggy bundle, a smile spreading over his handsome face as he watched the little twitching snout.

"Want to feed him?" Milly asked as she came in with a bottle of warmed milk.

"I'll try, not sure if I can remember how to bottle feed a baby... or a pig,' He joked.

"Can he have some garlic bread Milly?"

"No darling, he's too small. In a couple of weeks maybe."

Bill took the bottle and started feeding the greedy little fellow.

It was a picture of the purest domesticity, although the piglet made it look a bit surreal, but Milly felt as though her heart would burst with happiness.

Zac was asleep in bed and Milly and Bill were enjoying a quiet brandy when Ciara and Charlie came in. Laughing and giggling they went straight upstairs.

"Cheeky girl, she pinched my room," Bill joked.

"She did," Milly said, smiling.

An awkward silence ensued only broken when Bill took Milly's hand across the table.

"You are the loveliest landlady I've ever met; do you know that Milly Henderson?"

"And you are my most handsome guest."

The next moment, Bill pulled Milly close and they kissed. Luckily no one lost any teeth.

"Ciara," Charlie whispered. I've just seen My Dad and Milly go upstairs together. They're holding hands… You don't think...?"

"Nah, they're too old and your Dad's just had a heart attack."

"Yeah, He's probably checking some leak. There's loads in this house. They looked very friendly tho…"

"Thank God for my little life-savers," Bill murmured in Milly's ear as he unzipped her dress.

"Yes, thank God for them," Milly joked as she put her arms around him.

She had to be up early and cook breakfast for some guests but she didn't care.

Energy begets energy old girl…

Ever the gentleman, Bill insisted on helping her in the kitchen the next morning. Both were glowing as Milly cooked and he and Zac served the breakfast.

"Your Dad's looking very perky this morning," Ciara whispered to Charlie after Bill had given them some tea and toast.

"Dirty old dog," Charlie remarked, smiling.

Chapter Eighteen

"So, did the earth move?" Sasha asked excitedly.

"It did." Milly smiled on the other end of the phone.

"And what about the clacky teeth?"

"Everything stayed in place. Thank god."

"Oh Milly, this is so exciting. I must meet him."

"Definitely not. You might pinch him."

"It sounds as if he only has eyes for you."

"At the moment."

"What do you mean?"

"He's around a lot of women and travels a lot."

"Milly, he's not Jack."

"I know."

"Well then? What's wrong?"

"It all feels a bit too good to be true…"

"You just don't know how goddam beautiful you are my friend. You've always had men falling at your feet and were oblivious... No one understood how you got hooked up with Jack… Anyway, I mustn't speak ill of the dead…" Sasha knew how defensive Milly could get when Jack's name was mentioned.

Funny, Sasha reflected, *how so many of us only remember the good things about people when they die.*

"So, how is the delectable Sophie?" she asked brightly, keen to steer the conversation away from Jack.

"Blooming… but gearing up to be a single mother by the sound of it. She's having a girl by the way. She's going to call her Hope."

"Oh, Milly, that's so sweet."

"It is, isn't it?" Milly beamed.

"You've all got lots of good things to look forward to," Sasha remarked kindly. "Sophie will be okay. She is your daughter. And as for you and Bill. Well, you've both had your share of heartache my friend. I think this is your time."

It was.

In between tours, Bill was spending the majority of his time at 'Willow Cottage' with Milly. Charlie had finished his run at the 'Festival Theatre' and was on location in Ireland making a film. He and Ciara were still an item and had moved into Bill's London flat. So, Milly and Bill were effectively, living together.

"Milly," Bill said, putting his hand over hers one evening as they were eating in the dining room. "I want to marry you."

Milly's stomach did a loop.

"Marry me?"

"Yes, marry you."

"But Bill, do we actually need to get married? I mean we are fine as we are, aren't we?"

"Don't you want to marry me?"

"I just don't want to spoil things…"

And so life continued. They were blissfully happy. Bill kept asking but Milly still wouldn't tie the knot.

Chapter Nineteen

Thirteen years later.

Rufus didn't eat his breakfast again that morning. He just wasn't interested in food. A dejected sniff at his bowl and he padded back to his old basket by the Aga in the kitchen.

"Come on old boy, come and eat something," Milly tried to coax him as she bent down and stroked him in his basket. He lifted his tired eyes and looked at her, dolefully.

Mark, their vet, had gently told a weeping Milly and a stoic Bill earlier that week that they'd know when it was time to put an end to his suffering. Rufus was now eighteen years old and his great big heart was failing. He didn't even have the strength or inclination these days to greet the paper boy at the door and take Bill's morning paper to him in the dining room. Something he had done faithfully every morning since Milly and Jack had lived together. And truth be told, Bill had grown as fond of Rufus as Milly. In many ways, he was the baby they'd never had.

She was still stroking her faithful old companion as Bill came back into the kitchen.

"It's time isn't it my darling?" He said, bending down and putting his arm around Milly.

"You've had enough haven't you, old boy? I will call Mark," Bill said in a quiet voice.

"Yes, yes please Bill, I just can't make the call…"

"I know darling, it's okay, let me speak to them."

"Mark said he'd come to the house," Bill said as he came back into the kitchen.

"That's good of him,' Milly sniffed, "I don't think I could bear to take him in to the surgery."

The memories rolled back as Milly sat quietly at the kitchen table, staring at her faithful old companion of nearly twenty years.

The first day, Jack had brought Rufus into their house in Barnes, the boys were just three and five years old and Sophie was a babe in arms. Milly was furious. How was she supposed to cope with a puppy who was practically the same size as the boys? It was like having a mini horse in the house. And typical Jack, he hadn't said anything to her about getting a dog. Just gave her some sob-story about some guy in the pub who'd said his wife had thrown them both out of the house and that 'it was him or the dog…'

Milly said she'd give Rufus a week and if things were too stressful it would be Jack or the dog. Of course he raced around the house knocking over chairs and chewing toys but he was marvellous with the boys and developed a particular bond with Jake, who was going through quite a difficult time adjusting to school. When they went out for a walk to the duck pond in the village, people would stop and smile at the sight of two little boys holding on to his lead as he led them along in their double buggy. Rufus was the 'Pied Piper of Hamlin' trotting protectively at the helm of his little family.

Then there were the lonely nights in London when Milly sat motionless staring at the walls in their house, trying not imagine what Jack was up to with Magda. In many ways it was Rufus who saved Milly. If she'd had her way, she'd have stayed in bed all day watching day-time television and eating cheese sandwiches but Rufus had to go out for his daily walk, come rain or shine. It was him who made her get out of bed every morning and face the day. It was him who sat faithfully by her side, night after night when it was too late to call a friend, his head in her lap, tuning into her misery. It was him who protected her in 'Willow Cottage', sleeping in her bedroom in those early days before she met Bill. Checking out any dodgy looking guests at the door.

The doorbell rang and Bill let in Mark, who quietly sat down at the table opposite Milly. Taking her hand, he assured her that Rufus would just go gently to sleep.

"He won't feel a thing, Milly," he said quietly. "He will just close his eyes and drift off. It is the kindest thing."

"Yes, yes, I know Mark, thank you, I know."

The silence was crucifying and Milly just watched mutely as Mark opened his medical case and took out the dreaded syringe.

"Wait, wait just a moment," Milly said leaping out of her chair. "Can I just take him outside for a moment, into the garden?"

"Yes of course, take as long as you like."

"Darling, he may not have the strength," Bill interjected softly.

But Rufus managed to shuffle out into the back garden with Milly to 'Dad's' enclosure. 'Dad' was there poking his head through the fence waiting for his old pal. Milly opened the gate and Rufus painfully willed his body into the enclosure where he sank to the ground. 'Dad' waddled over and sat with him. This had been their morning ritual since 'Dad' had been a little piglet and the two were devoted to one another.

Mr O'Leary was right, 'Dad' had grown into a hefty fella over the years and was much happier when he was moved outside, into the garden and his own cosy shed. He'd soon learnt to open the baby gate Bill had erected in the dining room and would drag towels and sheets out into the hall. Next it would be the kitchen where he'd root around the bin, put his nose into plug sockets before knocking over tables and chairs in the dining room.

Not a good look for a nice, posh 'B&B'. Milly smiled at the memory.

"Would you like me to take a picture?" Bill suggested.

"No darling let's keep this memory just for us. We don't need any pictures to spoil the intimacy of their last moments together."

"I'll ask Mark to come out here."

"Yes, I'd like that."

Mark came out with his medical bag and put Rufus gently to sleep. 'Dad' wouldn't leave his side and sat protectively next to his old friend for the rest of the day.

They buried Rufus in the garden under the hazelnut tree, just outside 'Dad's' enclosure. 'Dad' still poked his nose through the fence waiting for his friend every morning and Bill had to cancel the daily delivery of his paper. It was just too painful not to have Rufus rush to the letterbox.

In time, maybe they'd get another dog.

***

"Here you are darling, 'G&T' time!" Milly chirped brightly, taking their drinks into the sitting room. "I've just been speaking to Sophie. My God, that girl is a worry. Hope stayed out late again last night, poor Sophie sounds at her wits end… Now darling, you haven't taken your pills?"

"Yes, I did my love. But you gave me an extra brown and blue one, so I've left them in the pot."

"Did I? Are you sure?" Milly frowned.

"Yes, darling. I take the damn things every day. Don't worry. No harm done."

"Okay, if you say so… anyway, as I was saying, poor Sophie…"

Bill suddenly dropped his drink and his head lolled to one side.

"Bill, darling, what's the matter? Bill, speak to me…" Mumbling and dribbling he was completely incoherent. Milly ran to the phone and called an ambulance.

"Please come quickly, it's my husband. He's trying to say something but I can't understand him, his face is lop-sided and I think he's had a stroke…"

Minutes later the ambulance shot up the drive. Two para-medics raced into the house, and as soon as they saw Bill, confirmed Milly's worst fears.

"Would you like to accompany us to the hospital?" the kindly, older one asked.

"Yes, yes of course," Milly stammered. Her heart in her mouth. I'll just get my handbag."

It was all horribly reminiscent. The klaxon blaring, swerving around corners in the ambulance, then being advised to wait in the quiet, more private waiting room at the hospital... always a bad sign… For Milly this was déjà vu. As she sat alone with her thoughts it all came flooding back. Jack had gone out jogging. Milly was in the kitchen loading the dishwasher after breakfast. Jenny, their neighbour knocked frantically at Milly's kitchen window. '*Milly, come quickly,' she'd said, 'Jack has collapsed. I've called an ambulance; the paramedics are with him. He's down the road…"*
Milly ran out of the house still wearing her rubber gloves. There he was, minus a trainer. Just lying there, seemingly lifeless on the ground. She went with him in the ambulance holding on to his discarded trainer.
Twenty minutes later, she was told that he died.

But that was then and this was now. Not knowing what to do with herself Milly paced the tiny room. After what seemed hours later, a kindly nurse led her into the wards where Bill was hooked up to monitors and various tubes. He was awake but couldn't speak which was very distressing for them both as he kept pointing to his mouth and shaking his head.

"Rest darling, everything will be okay, try to stay calm." Milly squeezed his hand.
A young Doctor came over and confirmed Milly's worst fears.

"Your husbands is doing very well but I can confirm that he has had a stroke. We will do further tests tomorrow Mrs Worsley and then we should have a clearer picture of how to progress with your husband's treatment."

Even though they weren't married Milly liked being

to as 'Mrs. Worsley' and readily referred to Bill in
conversations as 'her husband.'
She was petrified.
 "Please Bill, hold on darling. I think we should get
married. How nice would that be? We could have the
reception at 'Willow Cottage', have a lovely honeymoon
in Zanzibar, you always said you wanted to go there…"
Bill squeezed her hand and Milly cried.

 Three hours later she got a taxi home. It would have
been nice to have been welcomed by the familiar bark of
Rufus. She still missed her old faithful friend who always
knew when something was up. The grandfather clock was
ticking in the hall and the silence was deafening. Bill's gin
glass was lying on the floor, the empty tonic bottle on the
table by his chair. Waking around in circles Milly didn't
know what to do. The house was eerily silent.
Charlie… Oh God, I'll have to tell him.
But she couldn't bring herself to pick up the phone.

***

 The news wasn't good. Bill was paralysed down one
side and would effectively be bed-bound. Thankfully, he'd
regained the power of speech and a few days later he
surprised Milly by telling her the consultant had told him
that morning he would be allowed to go home the
following week.
In the meantime, Charlie had leapt into action; building
ramps from their bedroom into the sitting room and
widening door frames to adjoining rooms to allow for a
wheelchair to pass through.

***

 Everybody was there for Bill's homecoming. Charlie
and Ciara, Sophie and Hope, Zac, Ben and Jake. All of
whom Bill had got to know well over the years. Although
Norah, sadly, was no longer with them.

Wheeling his father into the sitting room, Charlie cracked open a bottle of champagne and rose his glass in a toast.

"Good to have you home, Dad."

"Thank you one and all," Bill replied "Now, I would like to propose a toast to Milly, who has been sitting by my side, every day in hospital." He raised his glass. "To Milly, the light of my life."

Milly had to turn away to hide her tears. Her handsome man, confined to a wheelchair. No more laughing in the kitchen together as they made breakfast for the guests. No more walks on the beach. No more wandering the aisles in Waitrose or pottering in the garden - all those little things that made up their life together.

***

Life settled into a predictable pattern. Carers came in twice a day to bath Bill and help with his personal care. He was a big man and there was no way Milly could get him out of bed and into the bathroom by herself. She was thankful for their help but was always terrified they would drop him from that awful contraption called a 'hoist', which was used to scoop him out of bed like a stork carrying a baby in a sling.

"Oh please, do be careful. Don't drop him!" This was a regular plea.

"Don't worry Milly, your husband will be fine. We are trained to use this equipment you know."

"Yes, I'm sure you are, but should he be dangling like that? Oh Lord, he's going to fall…"

Undaunted, Bill always laughed good naturedly.

"This is actually quite fun, my darling."

Naturally, the carers weren't amused and were clearly always hoping that Milly would just disappear and leave them to it.

"Milly darling, don't fret," Bill said, taking her hand after the carers had taken their leave and he was sitting up in bed as fresh as a newly bathed baby. "They know what they are doing."

"Do they?" Milly snapped. "They look about sixteen and only have three days training you know. We never know who's turning up apart from Danielle. She's the most reliable member of staff and if I hadn't have come in when I did, they would have dropped you."

"Well, they didn't and if they do, think of all that money we can sue them for?" Bill laughed.

"Oh, Bill," Milly stroked his cheek. "I'm sorry it's just…"

"You can't bear to see me like this..."
Milly was overcome with shame.

"I know. It's okay. I can speak and I can read. I can listen to my music. Unlike a lot of the other poor fellows in that ward."

"I know, darling, I know." Milly started to cry.

"Look, why don't you have a day out tomorrow? Go shopping with Sasha or see a film or something."

"No, no, I couldn't do that," Milly shook her head.

"Why not? I'm fine. The carers come in. I'm not going anywhere. If I'm worried about anything I can call you. I've got my phone… Go on, call Sasha or Sophie. You need a day out of this house."
Reluctantly, Milly agreed, called Sophie and arranged to meet her the next day for lunch in town.

***

"You look tired Mum."

"I'm okay darling." Milly was eating her ravioli at a snail's pace, all the while checking her phone in case there was a message from Bill.

"You've lost weight. You need to look after yourself you know."

"I know, I do," she answered distractedly.

"I can't stay long darling. I need to get back for Bill."

"Mum, I've driven an hour and a half to meet you. Try and have a nice time." Sophie snapped.

"I'm sorry Soph. It's just... I feel permanently on edge. You know, I worry that he might have fallen out of bed or something and he's there all alone in the house."

"Mum, stop it. He's fine. He's got his phone. He would call you."

"I know, darling. I'm sorry."

"So how is he adjusting?"

Milly's eyes filled with tears.

"Better than me. I feel so guilty sometimes. I'm the one who always seems to be snapping for no reason. And he has to sleep in that horrible bed."

"What do you mean?"

"It's a sort of air bed. Because he is paralysed it moves up and down to prevent him getting bed sores and makes an awful hissing sound. I miss him Soph, miss him sleeping in our bed."

"Oh Mum", Sophie put her hand over her mother's. "I bet you've had a lot more fun under the sheets than your single daughter has these last few years."

The joke passed Milly by.

"I'm sorry darling, I don't mean to rush you, but I really think we should get back and check on Bill."

"Okay mum," Sophie sighed. They'd been out just over an hour.

"You two were quick its only just two o'clock." Bill remarked as he looked up from his novel.

"Well, I tried to get her to go shopping but she just wouldn't have it." Sophie said, hugging Bill. "Can I get you a cup of tea?"

"Glass of wine or gin and tonic more like."

"But Bill, your medication?" Milly interjected.

"Oh poof, I take it with my wine when you aren't looking old girl. A glass of wine with your lovely daughter is just the tonic I need."

"Okay, well make it a small glass Soph. I'll leave you two alone for a bit while I go and check on the bookings."

"So how are you, dear girl?" Bill asked, patting his bed for Sophie to sit down." And how is that lovely little Hope behaving herself?

"Not working hard enough at school. Not the best circle of friends but other than that, okay. I guess it's just being a teenager."
Bill studied Sophie's face.

"These are very decisive years Sophie. If you are not happy with her school or the company she keeps, you have to change things."

"Easier said than done Bill."

"The answer is staring you in the face my dear. Move down here. It's a great area and the schools are good. You'd have your mother and me to support you and you know how fond we are of Hope and you. It would be a privilege. We need some young blood in this place."

They'd had this conversation numerous times. Both Bill and Milly had a bee in their bonnet about Sophie and Hope living in rented accommodation. They didn't think London was the right place to bring up a child and besides, Sophie was struggling both financially and emotionally. How many times Milly remarked, *'Living in that flat is one step forward for you Soph, and three back.'*

But Sophie wasn't ready to leave London, her job or her friends. She knew her mother and Bill wanted the best for her but moving back in with your parents when you were on the wrong side of thirty, with a bolshy teenager? Supposing everything went pear-shaped? Then she'd really be up shit creek.

"You need the security of bricks and mortar Sophie," Bill continued. "Your mother wants to make part of the house over to you and I would strongly advise you to accept her offer. The rest of the house can be sold off when Milly and I are no longer around and the proceeds go to your brothers. We know you like that flat of yours, dear girl, but it isn't really yours is it? What will happen when your landlord dies?"

Sophie was starting to feel stressed and didn't want to continue this conversation. Of course, she was incredibly grateful and felt very lucky to have this option but her mother and Bill both had this uncanny knack of making her feel really inadequate on occasion.

"Think about it Sophie, you need to think about your long-term security, besides, I'm worried about your mother…"

"You're worried about Mum?"

"Yes, I haven't said anything before but she's started to forget things. I'm sure it's the stress of looking after me but, to be frank, she's made a couple of mistakes administering my pills."

"Oh God Bill, are you sure?"

"Yes, my body may be giving up on me but my memory hasn't yet, thank God. I take the damn things every day, I know the dosage. She gave me an extra brown Warfarin tablet twice last week. Mistook it for one of the other little blue ones probably. She's done it a few times lately."

"Have the carers noticed anything?"

"No, I make sure they don't." Bill said knowingly. "We don't want that nosey Social Services lot poking their noses in do we?"

Sophie worried all the way home in the car. She couldn't keep this to herself. How on earth was she going to broach this with her mother? God forbid that she should give Bill an overdose.

I'll have to speak to the carers. Get them to take over the medication. Mum simply can't do it anymore.

A couple of days later, Milly rang Sophie.

"I've never been so humiliated in my life dear; those wretched carers are taking over the dispensing of all Bill's medication and I'm a trained nurse."

"Oh, is that such a bad thing Mum? At least you won't have to worry about dashing out for more pills anymore."

"Well, I think it's a bloody cheek. Anyone would think I was trying to poison him. Three years it took me to earn my stripes. And that was in a proper London hospital, when wards were run like ships. None of these so called, 'carers' have S.R.N after their name. Damn nerve. Anyway dear, on a happier note, I've some news for you."

"Oh, yes, good I hope?"

"Bill and I are getting married."

"Oh, Mum, that's fantastic. So, he finally got you to say yes, after all this time?"

"Yes, well, he says it would mean a lot to him."

"And you, I hope?"

"Oh yes dear, he's stuck with me this long, so better late than never."

"Well, I think it's great news and no doubt Charlie is thrilled."

"Yes, I think he is."

"So, when is the wedding?"

"Charlie and I are going into the registry office this week to pick a date."

Chapter Twenty

Bill hadn't been out of bed much at all since he came home from the hospital. Sometimes he allowed the carers to wheel him out into the garden in his wheelchair on a sunny day but much to Milly's disappointment, he hardly ever went into the adjoining sitting room, which was always his favourite place to sit with his glass of wine in front of the fire place.

But today was different.

The woman he had adored for so many years had finally agreed to become his wife.

He was all smiles as Charlie helped him out of bed and he looked as wickedly handsome as ever when Milly saw him in his morning suit. A yellow rosebud pinned in his lapel.

"Milly, my darling." he said, holding her hand as Charlie pushed him in his wheelchair out to the car. "You look beautiful. Every inch the bride."

An electric blue, silk dress and jacket stylishly complimented Milly's still lustrous, silver-grey hair, which was swept up into a French style chignon. While a silver pair of Jimmy Choo's and matching handbag completed her look.

"And you look as debonair as the first day you walked into this house," Milly smiled. "Now, are you going to get me to the church on time? We've got a wedding to go to."

All the village had heard about the wedding. Audrey, from 'Ye Old Sweet Shop 'B&B',' and the landlords from both the 'Woolpack' and 'Bulls Head' pubs came out to wave them on their way to their wedding. Jake drove them in a silver-grey Rolls Royce, specially decked out with flowers on the number plates by Sophie and Hope.

Zac, who was now a very handsome young man in his twenties rushed to open the car door for them when they arrived at the Registry Office. He adored both Milly and Bill and thought of them as his adopted grandparents.

"You both look really cool," he beamed.

"Thank you darling," Milly ruffled his hair.

"Oh Mum, you look gorgeous," Sophie kissed her mother, as she stepped out of the car.

"Your Mum has always been a stunner," Sasha remarked as she kissed her friend, confetti at the ready for after the ceremony.

"And you, my beautiful daughter and my dearest friend, both look lovely too… Ah, and there's my beautiful Hope," Milly squealed in delight.

She really is the image of my lovely Sophie, Milly observed with a glow in her heart.

"Hello Grandma, Grandad, you both look really great. I've got my confetti ready! Smile" she said, grabbing a quick selfie of them all altogether.

Charlie and Ciara, who had grown together very comfortably over the years were both incredibly excited about the wedding and both Ben and Jake had made it back from America to share this special day.

"Oh, my goodness, Bill, we must be the oldest bride and groom here," Milly joked as they made their way up the aisle.

"Patience is a virtue," Bill whispered.

"Better late than never," Milly smiled, squeezing his hand.

"And I now pronounce you man and wife," the Registrar announced as Bill slipped the wedding band on Milly's finger.

"I've been waiting fifteen years for his day," Bill joked as they kissed.

"Hip, hip hoorah," Zac called out, much to everyone's startled amusement.

As they stepped outside into the Chichester sunshine as Mr and Mrs William Worsley, Milly saw a face she thought she recognised. It was Magda, Zac's mother, looking at them from across the road. Zac and Sophie both looked horrified when they spotted her.

"Oh my God, what's she doing here?" Sophie whispered.

"Mum, what are you doing?" Zac mouthed to his mother, across the road. Both tried to stop Milly from going over to speak to her. But, for some reason, Milly felt compelled to go.

"Milly," Magda said, with a tear in her eye as she clutched Milly's hand. "I just wanted to witness your happy day. I am so happy you found love again."

"Oh, Magda, why don't you join us. Zac is here."

"No, no Milly, I can't. Zac would be furious with me. I don't want to spoil your day."

"You won't be spoiling anything. Come on, Zac can drive you to the restaurant. We're just going to have a spot of lunch."

"No, I just wanted to catch a glimpse of you and wish you every happiness. You will never know how sorry I am for causing you so much sorrow Milly."

Milly could sense that this was something that Magda had wanted to say for a very long time. She had lost her youthful bloom and age didn't sit comfortably with her.

"Magda, having Zac in our lives has more than made up for everything and life does move on."

"Thank you, Milly," she said drying her eyes. Zac wouldn't be the wonderful boy he is without you and I thank you for that. I have to go now."

Before Milly could say anything, Magda hurried away to a waiting car.

Zac crossed the road and walked over to Milly as his mother was walking away. "Milly, are you alright? I had no idea my mother would show up like that. What did she want?" he was beside himself with embarrassment.

"It's okay, Zac, really. She was nice. Really nice…"

Zac looked thoroughly perplexed as they linked arms and walked back to the Registry Office. Sophie immediately pounced on him, looking worried.

"Who was that Milly?" Bill asked.

"Just a well-wisher darling. Tell you all later."

"How nice, come on, we need to pose for some photographs to prove we actually did this."

As the sun smiled on this happy couple and their friends and family showered them with a confetti of fragrant rose petals, Milly reflected on how strange life could be. She always thought she'd couldn't survive without Jack. And now here she was, a bride again, at seventy-three.

While the guests took their places for lunch at the 'Angel Hotel', Bill leaned over and took Milly's hand.

"Are you happy Mrs Worsley?" Bill asked, holding her with his still twinkly, brown eyes.

"Yes, very. Moving to 'Willow Cottage' was the best thing I ever did. It brought us together didn't it? My predecessor was right, it was a very lucky move for me."

"And us," Charlie smiled, putting his arm around Ciara.

"You know Soph," Bill said tenderly, as he reached for Sophie's hand, "We all think a move to 'Willow Cottage' could be very lucky for you too."

***

End of Book Two

AFTERWORD

'Willow Cottage' is a seventeenth century ex-coaching inn, school and brothel which my mother, Sheila, ran very successfully as a 'Bed and Breakfast' establishment for thirty-odd years. Many of the stories in both 'Sunny Side Up' and 'The Bed and Breakfast Queen', are based on her experiences living and working in the house.

She had a pot-bellied pig called Polly, who lived in the garden. I have fond memories of us all feeding her with a baby bottle when she was a piglet. We'd hold her close, like a tiny babe in arms swaddled in a blanket, her tiny little snout twitching. She didn't stay small for long and soon grew into a hefty great girl, charging around my mother's sitting room knocking over magazine racks. My mum took great care of her, feeding her apples and plums from the garden and scratching her back with a broom - something Polly adored.

Like Rufus, Polly was great friends with my mum's dog, Jane, an extremely soppy but ferocious looking Bullmastiff who is buried in the garden. When Polly died at the grand old age of sixteen, we placed a specially commissioned statue of a black pig sitting on a little pedestal in the back garden close to Jane's grave.

'Polly the pig' was cremated at the local pet cemetery and my mum still has her ashes in a sealed wooden box.

Audrey, the 'B&B Queen' at the 'Old Sweet Shop' is a fictional character. All the 'B&B' people my mum knew were quite delightful – as are the landlords and landladies in the 'Woolpack Inn' and 'Bull's Head' Pub opposite 'Willow Cottage'.

The Bookie, Mr O'Leary, is modelled on a real guest who stayed at 'Willow Cottage' every year. A grand old fella, he used to delight my mum with his stories about fraternising with various seedy characters in London's once notorious East End. He did indeed turn up one year on a stretcher with his two minders.

I'm sorry to say, that Mr Ponytail existed. He and his girlfriend went to great pains to befriend my mother and grandmother. One night they cleared off with a prized Victorian doll, some valuable Toby jugs and other treasured possessions and he had no qualms about leaving his false ponytail and stick-on tattoos in the waste paper basket in his room.
His mermaid lady-friend is a fictional character based on a real-life 'Mer-person.' A charming lady, she would never be involved with a scum-bag like Mr Ponytail!

The American posing as a bereaved husband and father is based on a real trickster, known to Sussex Police who conned my mother and stepfather out of a substantial amount of cash when they found him sobbing in the dining room one morning. As my step-father rushed out for the brandy this guest told them that his wife and daughter had been killed in a car crash in America during the night. Extremely upset for him, they didn't charge for his stay and paid for a taxi to take him to Gatwick Airport along with some cash.

Miss Gibbons is a fictional character although my mum did experience several other ghostly encounters in the house. Like Milly's guests, a couple staying with my mum were adamant they spotted a white-faced lady with long dark hair at their bedroom window as they came back to the house one evening.

When writing 'Sunny Side Up,' I tried to touch on some of the problems many people face today. Problems such as loneliness, disappointment and betrayal in love. Lack of money at a time in your life when you least expect it.

I hope 'Sunny Side Up' will inspire all the wonderful, more mature men and women out there who may have hung their hats up on love.

Just remember, don't worry about any clacky teeth!

Coming Soon

Book Three of
'The Willow Cottage Trilogy'

'MOVING ON'

Milly is getting older.
She worries about her daughter Sophie, a single parent living in
London on a shoe-string, with a wayward daughter.
Surely it makes more sense for them all to live together in
'Willow Cottage'? Her daughter could step into her shoes and
make a nice comfortable living, allowing Milly to take a back
seat and grow old gracefully, safe in the knowledge that her
daughter has her own home.

But is Milly as ready as she thinks to hand over the
reins of her precious 'B&B'?
And could Sophie live with the increasingly erratic
behaviour of her mother?

Published on Amazon in 2019

Also by Clare Cassy

TWO OF A KIND

How many chances does one person have to find true love?
When Juanita Estevez' path crosses with Santi Alverez,
a world-famous fashion photographer who rudely snaps a picture
of her when she is out shopping, their worlds are turned upside
down as they come to realise that they are *Two of a Kind*.
Both are fiercely ambitious, passionate and supremely
talented at what they do.
But having a talent often has its price.
Can they ever get together and if so, how?

Available on Amazon.com as an eBook or Paperback

Reader Ratings: 4.7 out of 5 Stars

Reviews for 'Two of a Kind'.

*'Two of a Kind is a happy love story filled with many unexpected
twists and turns. It reminded me a lot of an international and
modern twist on Pride and Prejudice.*
*The two main characters are incredibly ambitious, and
considering the short timeline within the book (less than a year for
sure), I felt like the character's stories were developed very well'.*
-Lemondrop. (Amazon) 2018

***

*'The book has a very easy-to-follow storyline that many would
enjoy reading while on holiday, or anyone looking for a brief
escape from the mundane aspects of everyday life.*
*I would recommend this book to anyone looking to read a
cheerful story.'*

Reviews for 'Two of a Kind' (cont.)

***

*'Every girl's dream, story full of passion, jealousy, travel,
fashion, riches and triumph.
Loved every moment - a must read.'*

***

'Heart-warming with a sense of innocence. A lovely read.'

***

*'Such a lovely and gripping romance between the main
characters. A heart-warming story about following your dreams
and falling in love - and all the bumps along the way.
A fantastic read!'*

Titles available on Amazon.com as an eBook or Paperback

By Clare Cassy

'The Willow Cottage Trilogy'
Book 1

THE BED AND BREAKFAST QUEEN

The Willow Cottage Series begins with Holly Bradbury, a disillusioned 30-something writer, questioning the life she has made for herself with her partner in their busy, so-called glamorous careers in magazines and advertising.
When an opportunity to change her life presents itself in the form of an advert for 'Willow Cottage', Holly jumps in feet first to become a *'Bed and Breakfast Queen.'*

Read about her adventures with unpredictable guests, an eccentric cleaning lady, a massive dog and an exciting stranger, as she discovers being a *'Bed and Breakfast Queen'* can be frustrating, moving and sometimes just plain hilarious.

***

'I loved this book and so did my daughter. Great read and I highly recommend it. When I got to Chapter 9, I was so into the story I simply had to read till the end.
We can't wait for the next book.'

www.clarecassy.co.uk

Facebook.com/ClareCassyAuthor

Twitter
@cassy_clare

Titles available on Amazon.com as an eBook or Paperback

46304174R00081

Printed in Poland
by Amazon Fulfillment
Poland Sp. z o.o., Wrocław